OPEN CITY

New York City, 1998
Number Six

PRAVDA   281 Lafayette Street 226.4696

LEO CASTELLI

420 WEST BROADWAY
578 BROADWAY
NEW YORK

OPEN CITY

THE EASTERN & ORIENTAL RESTAURANT
WITH
THE SUZIE WONG LOUNGE

THAI AND VIETNAMESE CUISINE
NOON - 3 AM • FREE DELIVERY
100 WEST HOUSTON AT THOMPSON, NYC • 254.7000

OPEN CITY

EDITORS
Thomas Beller
Daniel Pinchbeck

SENIOR EDITORS
Robert Bingham
Elizabeth Schmidt

ART DIRECTOR
Meghan Gerety

EDITOR-AT-LARGE
Adrian Dannatt

CONTRIBUTING EDITORS
Will Blythe
Amanda Gersh
Thea Goodman
Kip Kotzen
Elizabeth May
Jim Merlis
Lee Smith
Lee Smith
Jon Tower

EDITORIAL ASSOCIATE
Alexandra Tager

PUBLISHER
Robert Bingham

OPEN CITY is a non-profit journal of the arts.
Subscription rate is $32 for four issues; institution rate, $40. Make checks payable to The Segue Foundation. *Mail to: OPEN CITY 225 Lafayette Street, suite 1114, New York, NY 10012. E-mail: dpinchbeck@aol.com*

Special thanks to Margaret Longbrake.
Cover photograph: Adam Fuss, *Untitled,* 1993
Title page illustration: Matthew Ritchie

ISBN 1-890447-17-x
ISSN 1-890-5523

LINCOLN PLAZA CINEMAS

Six Screens

63rd Street & Broadway
opposite Lincoln Center
757-2280

CONTRIBUTORS' NOTES

MARGARET PARK BRIDGES won the Suntory Award for Mystery Fiction in 1992 for her novel, *My Dear Watson*, which was published in Japan. She has also won the Academy of American Poets prize. She lives in Hopedale, Massachusetts, with her husband and two daughters, and is the author of three children's books, forthcoming from Morrow Jr. Books.

MICHAEL CUNNINGHAM is author of the novels *A Home At the end of the World* and *Flesh and Blood*.

ADAM FUSS's cover photograph was made in 1993.

DEBORAH GARRISON is a senior editor at the *New Yorker*. Her first book of poems, *A Working Girl Can't Win*, has just been published by Random House.

REM KOOLHAAS collaborated with Bernard Chang, Mihai Craciun, Nancy Lin, Yuyang Liu, Katherine Orff, Stephanie Smith, Marcela Cortina and Jun Takahashi on *Pearl River Delta, China*. He is one of the founders of the Office for Metropolitan Architecture based in Rotterdam and is the author of several books including: *S,M,L,XL* and *Delirious New York*.

ELLEN HARVEY lives and works in New York City. She recently had her first solo show at the Alexandre de Folin Gallery in Chelsea.

HUNTER KENNEDY fact-checks at *New York* magazine where he is known as the "inaccurate date." A native of Columbia, South Carolina, Kennedy is also the founder, editor and publisher of "The Minus Times."

MONICA LEWINSKY is based in Washington, D.C.

ERIC LINDBLOOM is a photographer whose work is represented by Gallery 292 in New York City. His study of Florence, *Angels at the Arno* (David R. Godine), was published in 1994.

SEAN McNALLY is a writer and wedding minister who lives in Milwaukee, Wisconsin. A recipient of this year's Milwaukee County Arts Fellowship, he has published his work in numerous literary gazettes and performed at spoken word venues across the United States. He is a frequent guest on Wisconsin Public Radio's "Hotel Milwaukee" program and is included in *The United States of Poetry*, companion book to the PBS television series. He is currently at work on his first novel.

DAVID MEANS is the author of a collection of stories entitled *A Quick Kiss of Redemption*, published by William Morrow. His short fiction has most recently appeared in *Harper's* magazine and *The Paris Review*.

RICK MOODY is the author of *The Ring of the Brightest Angels Around Heaven* (1995), a collection of stories, and the novels *Purple America* (1997), *The Ice Storm* (1994), and *Garden State* (1992), recently rereleased by Back Bay Books with a fine introduction by the writer involving his obsession with The Feelies. He lives in Brooklyn.

JAMES PURDY's most recent novel is *Gertrude of Stony Island Avenue*. The story in this issue is from a collection of short fiction to be published this autumn.

MATTHEW RITCHIE lives and works in New York. His most recent project was seen at the 1997 Biennial at the Whitney Museum of American Art and will be seen in 1998 in one-person shows at the Nexus Center for the Contemporary Arts in Atlanta, the Fundacia Cultural in Brazil, and Basilico Fine Arts in New York.

RICHARD ROTHMAN's work is represented in the collections of the Museum of Modern Art, La Bibliotheque Nationale de France, and other museum collections. His most recent show was at the Serge Sorokko Gallery in New York.

STRAWBERRY SAROYAN's work has appeared in *The Daily Telegraph*, *The Sunday Express*, and in *Personals: Dreams and Nightmares from the Lives of Twenty Young Writers*, forthcoming this summer from Houghton Mifflin. She lives in Los Angeles.

CHARLIE SMITH is the author of four books of poems, the latest of which is *Before and After*, published by Norton. The poems in this issue are from a forthcoming book called *Kansas*. He has also published six works of fiction, including *Cheap Ticket to Heaven* and *Shine Hawk*.

IVAN SOLATAROFF's essays and reportage have appeared in the pages of *The Villiage Voice* and *Esquire*. He is at work on a book about executioners.

CINDY STEFANS is an artist based in New York.

WILLIAM WENTHE received a poetry grant from the National Endowment for the Arts. His book *Birds of Hoboken* was published by Orchises Press and he has published poems in *Poetry* and the *Southern Review*. He teaches at Texas Tech University.

JOCKO WEYLAND is an artist and writer. His stories have appeared in *Thrasher*, *Ben is Dead*, and the anthology *Concrete Jungle*, published by Juno books. He is represented by the Steffany Martz Gallery.

SONNABEND

420 West Broadway
New York, New York 10012

ARTFORUM

STEFFANY MARTZ

529 West 20th Street 6th floor New York, NY 10011
t:212.206.3686   f:212.206.3654

Lunch • Dinner
301 Church Street, New York City
212 431 1445

GREENE NAFTALI

526 WEST 26TH STREET 8TH floor
NEW YORK, NEW YORK 10001

**"your mother
says I act like
your fairy
godmother"**
(Purdy, p.145)

PAULA COOPER GALLERY

534 West 21st Street New York, New York 10011
TEL 212.255.1105 FAX 212.255.5156

"...thick black leather pants, boots, and a biker jacket over a sawed-off black T-shirt featuring a human skull, humanoid figures, two salmon, and the credo SPAWN TILL YOU DIE; a tiny skull with a ruby eye pierces his left nipple."

(Solataroff, p.97)

An Idle Thought

Deborah Garrison

I'm never going to sleep
with Martin Amis
or anyone famous.
At twenty-one I scotched
my chance to be
one of the seductresses
of the century,
a vamp on the rise through the ranks
of literary Gods and military men,
who wouldn't stop at the President:
she'd take the Pentagon by storm
in halter dress and rhinestone extras,
letting fly the breasts that shatter
crystal—then dump him, too,
and break his power-broker heart.

Such women are a breed apart.
I'm the type
who likes to cook—no,
really likes it; does the bills;
buys towels and ties;
closes her eyes during kisses:
a true first wife.
The seductress when she's fifty
nobody misses, but a first wife
always knows she's first,
and the second (if he leaves me

when he's forty-five) won't forget me
either. The mention of my name,
the sight of our son—his and mine—
will make her tense; despite
perfected bod, highlighted hair
and hip career, she'll always fear
that way back there
he loved me more
and better simply
for being first.

But ho:
the fantasy's unfair to him,
who picked me young and never tried
another. The only woman he's ever left
was his mother.

Father, R.I.P., Sums Me Up at Twenty-Three

Deborah Garrison

She has no head for politics,
craves good jewelry, trusts too readily,

marries too early. Then
one by one she sends away her friends

and stands apart, smug sapphire,
the answer to everything a slender

zero, a silent shrug—and every day
still hears me say she'll never be pretty.

Instead she reads novels; instead her belt
matches her shoes. She is master

of the condolence letter, and knows
how to please a man with her mouth:

Good. Nose too large, eyes too closely set,
hair not glorious blonde, not her mother's red,

nor the glossy black her younger sister has,
the little raven I loved best.

A Friendship Enters Phase II

Deborah Garrison

We were sitting on the porch
after dinner, grown-ups taking
stock, no chance of our stopping:

we were going to stay up all night.
"We're going to stay up all night,"
one of us said, and you lit another cigarette

with a lazy flair,
like we'd just been in bed,
but our love was pure; I'd never

talked like that to anyone before.
Two fathers, one husband,
three would-be lovers were duly sworn

and testified before us in their turn;
their crimes were numerous;
when we peered down their gun barrels

their faces and hands and eyes glinted
and winked maddeningly at the other end.
And we were mad—mad to shake the kaleidoscope

again: even virginity, that shoeless waif,
streaked low across the moonless cloudlake like
a slip blown from the line and carried off

to rest in some stranger's muddy yard.
All, please: we'd tell no less, no stone
was left, etc... You were the maestro,

twirling a smoke in the dark,
then piping on it, braving the toy
puffs of death, conducting the ragtag band

of losses. "But why," you asked,
"didn't he love *me?*" Your deep laugh
dissolved into the peopled space between

the summer trees, whose black leaves flickered green
as morning came—the bitch!—to shut us down.
Goodbye, perfect night. You raised

your empty dinner glass to toast
our forward march, and tossing back
invisible shots we proceeded
backward into the light.

" 'Hi,' I say."
(Park-Bridges, p.47)

Burrito

Jocko Weyland

JASON KNEW THAT SOME KIND OF INCIDENT WAS IMMINENT THE moment the tattooed monster crossed the threshold into the small space in front of the counter. The other customers shrank away as the monster ordered his food. He was overconfident, full of bluster, and trying desperately to project toughness and hardness. Even though it was a laughable display it was working to a certain degree. His overly articulated physique, the convict appearance, the fawning sidekick with him, his impatient manner—they were all an invitation and a provocation to any small offense. That he thought he shouldn't have to wait was clearly evident. He ordered two burritos without beans and stepped back to edgily bide his time.

He came in at a time when people could get despicable. A need for immediate gratification pushed their baseness to the surface. This impatience made for embarassing displays, unpleasant demonstrations of humankind at its pettiest. It was almost a war. They wanted their lunch served with alacrity and if it wasn't, overwrought responses were often unleashed—from yelling and screeching to pleading and threatening. All for some inauthentic serviceable Mexican food made in nearly fast-food time. These reactions came from people who appeared to be perfectly nice, normal citizens. They were closer to outbreaks of ugliness than their benign exteriors betrayed. The monster was past that breaking point before he even walked through the door. He didn't need time to get frustrated. He'd already run down the steps to the subway platform and seen the lights of his train receding into the tunnel. He telegraphed his impending eruption by the way he took up physical space, by just being. The space behind the counter where Jason

27

stood was cramped, the whole room measured twelve by twenty feet. Almost all of it was taken up by kitchen equipment—steamers and grillers, hot storage for meat and beans, a cold storage table for tomatoes, lettuce, jalapenos, and chips, a refrigerator for beer and soda. There was a tiny bathroom in the back and a sink and a little counter where the food was bagged. At higher levels were shelves stacked with boxes, plastic cups and aluminum food containers. Passageways barely a foot wide made a horseshoe shape through all the accoutrements of food preparation. The scarcity of space evoked a prison cell, a debilitating thwarting of movement.

A narrow counter with two cash registers bisected the area between this cage and the outside world. On the other side of the counter was a small triangular compartment for the patrons; it was only a few feet wide and bordered by the door and a large window looking out onto the sidewalk. There was a small shelf for eating on, three stools and two posters showing the various peppers of the world in color, with a potency rating of spiciness for each one. The triangle was stunted and close and when it filled up with people it got too cosy. It was like being in an elevator. Fine when there were only a couple of customers but increasingly uncomfortable with each new person. And unlike an elevator everyone didn't follow social convention and face the same way. The workers and the customers were face to face across the meager counter. Sometimes conflict arose in this hot sweaty elevator that wasn't going anywhere. They were in a hurry, their tempers rising, and the workers were doing their best while not being too concerned and were apt to rebel with sarcasm and a lackadaisical attitude. When the battle was joined it could get unfriendly.

It wasn't always like that. When Jason arrived in the morning the little space was empty and serene and as clean as it ever got. Its deep-rooted smell, which clung to the body for hours after a day of work, was at its lowest ebb; a pale odor at this point, slightly altered and alleviated by the disinfectant from the night before. Jason would put the money drawer in the register and turn the lights on to the sound of the ventilation fan lazily starting up. Once a week the first things to be dealt with were the dead and dying mice caught in the glue traps that had been left out overnight. Either cold and truly dead or half alive, squishy and still

28

warm. They lay hidden to be discovered—like finds in a morbid Easter egg hunt—and then thrown in the trash. Usually though it was mild setting up and making miniature sandwiches out of two tortilla chips with some cheese and a jalapeno pepper as filling, drinking Coca-Cola out of a brown plastic cup, and going out on the sidewalk to smoke a cigarette. The street would be un-crowded and sedate; Jason would daydream as the moments ticked past and indolently killed time.

Handsome with smooth, copper-brown skin, long hair and a trace of a mustache, Tony was a Dominican born in the city and the manager of the take-out. He was four years younger than Jason, almost a teenager but with a manner that made him seem older. He was at ease, confident and possessed an innate knowledge of urban life that Jason envied and admired. Tony was slyly curious and interested in the things Jason knew about, the residue of a college education and extensive travels, and Jason was learning from Tony about the city and its Byzantine social customs and un-familiar mores. Tony also had a comic side and an incredibly accurate talent for mimicry—of ethnic stereotypes, celebrities, and customers as soon as they walked out the door. They were com-fortable with each other and fed off of their respective differences. Jason would bring a small backgammon board and when it was slow they would open it on a stool behind the counter and play, withdrawing from the world in the warmth of nascent friendship and simple competitive pleasures.

Sergio and Jesus would arrive a little later in the morning. They were the Mexican cooks. What they did really wasn't cooking, they were preparators. They put out a tortilla, tossed some meat, beans, and cheese in, put that in a steamer for a minute, then finished off with the cold ingredients before wrapping the tortilla up and putting a lid on the aluminum foil dish they went in. Theirs was an economy of motion, a graceful dolloping of some sour cream here followed by a practiced sprinkling of the right amount of lettuce or peppers there. They were somewhat conversant in English and doggerel dialogue was constantly going on—Spanish to Spanish between Tony, Sergio and Jesus, their broken English countered by Jason's underdeveloped Spanish, and standard English competing via Tony and Jason's conversation. A Spanglish

Babel infused with laughter, a shared good-humored exasperation with their hopefully temporary lot.

Besides the cooks and Tony and Jason there were the bike delivery guys. Two from Bangladesh, two Poles, three Americans and one Puerto Rican. They rotated but in the day it was almost always Khaled and Saleem. Their relationship verged on being a vaudeville act. Khaled was mischievous and extroverted while Saleem took the pensive and serious role, the contrast leading to cub up routines in excited and speedy Bengali. As uncannily cliché as it seemed, they both had the goal of becoming taxicab drivers.

In a way their job was enviable. They got better tips and were free to roam the city and explore its geography while seeing fleeting instants of other people's lives, see them naked, their existences and intimacies exposed to the anonymous deliverer for the time it took to hand over a bag of food. They could imagine and dream other realities from these brief encounters. But it had its drawbacks, especially in the winter. Jason's jealousy waned as he watched Khaled and Saleem set out against the frigid wind off the river or come back soaked from snow, covered in slush, their fingers frozen blue with icicles forming on their mustaches. On these days the customers tipped less; out of maliciousness or more probably as a reflection of the weather's depressive effect of the psyche, translated to their purse strings.

All of the delivery guys shared one fear unanimously. It was being sent with an order to David Croudos' apartment. He ordered two or three times a week and when he did it was like Russian roulette, the loser in the cruel lottery having to make the delivery. He did sound creepy on the phone and was a poor tipper but it was nothing compared to the descriptions, brought back by the unfortunate messengers, of a stench appalling in its resplendence, in its evocation of rot, death and decay. They dreaded going there and their fear and revulsion betrayed an almost primal superstition. They were all visibly relieved upon each return from this apartment of horror.

There were two bike guys who didn't last very long. A new employee showed up one day to do deliveries. He was tall and sturdily built and dressed in overalls and clunky boots. He looked like a farmer straight off the tractor, a little out of place, and he had a southern drawl and drooping, sleepy eyelids. The only thing missing was a stalk of wheat between his teeth. He seemed amiable enough and was sent off with his first batch of orders. An hour and a half later he showed up. He had the bicycle but none of the sixty dollars that he was supposed to get for the food. He was also slower and practically somnambulistic. His eyes drooped even further and he didn't appear to be too concerned with explaining where the money was or where he had been. He went down to the basement and passed out. He had scored some heroin, showing that junkies come in the most unlikely packages. He was let go.

More innocent and less willfully subversive was the friend of Khaled and Saleem who showed up one day. He had just arrived from Bangladesh and couldn't speak any English. He was out of his element and scared, the look in his eyes was that of a deer inching up to a salt lick, ready to bound away at the first sign of danger. But he couldn't run away and on that fine fall day he was sent off with his first order. After an hour Jason and Tony were wondering aloud, "Where's the new guy?" He finally showed up and when questioned looked at Khaled and Saleem pleadingly. They made assurances that he had just gotten lost this one time and would get the hang of it.

He was given another order. A few seconds later Jason looked up the street and saw him walking the bike. Then he got on it and shakily attempted to pedal. He went a few feet, tottered, and fell off. He tried again and went a few more feet before toppling over. Then he started pushing the bicycle. Tony had joined Jason and they both watched, silently comprehending the real problem. He didn't know how to ride a bicycle. When he got back he was discharged by the restaurant manager who Jason and Tony had told, somewhat reluctantly, about his lack of skills. They were both laughing while simultaneously ruminating about the hell of confusion they knew the recent arrival must have been going through. Not knowing the streets, trying to decipher the foreign scrawl on the ticket, pushing the metal machine he had no idea of how to use. They took it for granted but how could he have ever known? His incomprehension and loss of balance weren't his fault.

Sometimes Jason had to descend through the trap metal doors

in the sidewalk to the basement to get supplies. The ceiling was low, it was always hot and crowded with boxes of bags and aluminum food containers, stacks of beer and soda and cannibalized bicycles. Down there he was instantly in solitary confinement and felt like a stowaway in the hold of a ship. One particularly sultry night he had to stay below longer than usual—it had been busy and a lot of goods had to be replenished upstairs. He was sweaty and his arms felt stretched out from carrying heavy loads up the rotting wooden stairs. Finally around midnight he was finished and went across the street to the subterranean office to count out the night's earnings. The manager that night was from the restaurant's other location; Jason had just met him. He was about forty and wan and bitter, and he exuded an air of having been repeatedly demoralized by the city. In the cramped space they sat knee to knee counting out the money, shiny with perspiration and funky with the smell of the food and grime.

As they counted the manager began a desultory ramble about the ills of the city and its quickening descent into depravity. His railing was scathing and all-encompassing, and as it went on he took on the aura of a messianic prognosticator of the coming apocalypse. Jason was so tired he just listened and nodded assent. The manager cited example after example, reaching an almost apoplectic state when he related his final indictment. Recently his neighbor, an old Polish immigrant, had been beaten and robbed in his apartment. Then his tormentors had poured gasoline over him and set him on fire, killing him. As he finished he stared off into space past Jason, the fire and brimstone drained out of him. Jason got out and onto the street and tried to taste the fresh air but the tortured and charred old man stayed with him for a long time past that night.

But on a clear fall day a little later there was no sign of the imminent melt-down of society. There was no conflict or danger. The street outside was placid and uncrowded, unhurried under the bleaching of the sun. Jason and Tony set up and then ate a meal, one of the endless combinations that they concocted using one of the four basic building blocks—the burrito, the enchilada, the quesadilla, and the taco. A burrito with chicken and extra cheese or a enchilada with mole sauce and sour cream or tacos with no meat and extra jalapenos or a quesadilla with beef, chicken, rice, salsa, sour cream and some added red sauce. In its infinite variety of combinations and numbing overall taste it blended together so it seemed like they never had eaten anything else. It was free, and for breakfast, lunch, and dinner. And with it came the smell that occupied the body and the olfactory senses, always reminding them of the never-changing fare and the job that went with it.

The lunch rush began, banishing boredom with sheer volume of manual repetitive tasks. The phone started ringing, Jason would ask for the address, phone number and order (with the very important special instructions) in rapid succession. The reply for how long it would take would invariably be answered with "Can't it be faster?" Then he would tear the ticket off the pad and slip it into place in a small metal crevice over where the cooks worked. With the people that walked in he would ask their name and write it on the slip so they could be called for when their order was done. Often he and Tony guessed or estimated the name they wrote on the slip, or when it got busy invented monikers—"Blue hat" or "Tweaker" that facetiously and succinctly described the person. There were regulars. The gay man who was one of their favorite and friendliest customers who they had dubbed "Peter Jesus" for some forgotten reason. Or the dottily inebriated former television comedy actress who always carried her toy poodle. Pretty women, handsome men. Fleeting meetings and imaginings across the counter consisting of light banter and innuendo and predictable jokes about the anti-flatulence bean additive they sold. The operation hummed along, Tony and Jason symbiotically laboring and laughing.

Into this fairly cheery scene walked the two men. One was white, muscular and pumped-up. His arms and part of his neck were covered with indistinguishable tattoos. He radiated animosity and ill will, like Popeye's nemesis come to life. His companion was black, smaller, and a lot skinnier. He walked in and inhabited the space right behind and to the side of the larger man, his manqué shadow. Together they were a caricature of the bloodthirsty duos that pillage through movies set in those lawless days that follow nuclear annihilation.

At first their antagonism could be ignored. There were too

many other things happening. The phone ringing, taking money and giving change, bagging orders. The tattooed man had to wait a while before he and his cohort stepped up to the register to order. He did so in a peremptory fashion, brusquely specifying that the two burritos had to be absolutely devoid of beans. The shadow was silent. Jason's eyes met theirs for the first time, there was an ocular transmission of arbitrary hostility coming from both of them. After the exchange of money they went to the corner and brooded.

Compulsively Jason's eyes kept drifting over to the corner at the insipid tattoos. They would travel up the messy and badly inked canvases and meet the eyes that were looking right at his. Jason took more orders and went about his business but he kept being drawn by some magnetic force to those arms and eyes. It became a staring contest, a test of wills. And each time the exasperation and impatience exhibited in those confrontational orbs grew. They accused Jason of purposely delaying the production of the food. Then the man would confirm his displeasure by rolling his eyes for his little friend, who would smirk towards Jason in agreement.

As the minutes passed the other customers became a mute audience, almost absent. It was just the enemy and Jason and Tony. Jason instinctively knew that Tony sensed what was going on, how things had gone beyond a typical case of customer annoyance to a real face-off; one in which there were innocent bystanders who weren't aware of what was going on. The heat and steam along with the inexplicable hate turned the atmosphere miasmatic. Jason couldn't think of anything else. He had only been in the city a short while and hadn't fought in a long time. Now adrenaline had clandestinely seeped into his whole body. He was scared.

Jason heard the snap of a bag being opened behind him and then Tony's voice.

"Tattoo . . . here you go." Jason had prophetically written "Tattooed Monster" on the slip before the situation had escalated. The bag was handed over and immediately inspected. Opening up one of the containers he asked angrily, "Does this have beans in it?" Tony calmly took a look, using a plastic knife to fold back a flap of burrito to expose some black beans. Tony apologized for the mistake and said it would be fixed. An emphatic "Jesus Christ!" exploded from the tattooed man as he rolled his eyes again and then glowered at Jason. His suspicions had been confirmed. He was pissed and wanted everybody in the vicinity to know, to understand that Jason and Tony's stupidity had led to a colossal blunder that was going to prevent him from doing something very, very important.

The couple returned to their corner of disservice while Tony turned to the cooks and instructed them in Spanish to hurry up with the correct order. Now Tony was involved in the conflict, a triangle of antagonistic sight lines formed between Tony and Jason and the two skulking figures in the corner. Jason peripherally interpreted a glance from Tony that meant "Whatever…it's cool" while the monster's muscles rippled and the veins in his neck became more prominent. Awakened to the situation, the other customers stood still and quietly studied their shoes. There was a combination of dread and expectancy. Would Tony and Jason produce the right assemblage of flour tortillas and various other ingredients before they got physically attacked? The phone kept ringing, Jason answered and took orders with an unnaturally controlled voice. Tony kept snapping bags open and filling them, nonchalantly smiling and handing them to customers who turned with relief and slipped out the door. With every person who got their food the mimed display of rage in the corner became more performative. His face really was getting red. The sidekick did his best to look disgusted and potentially violent. Time slowed down, just eyes to eyes, the sounds of chips dryly crackling, meat sizzling, the dull bang of a spoon against metal.

Then the dam burst. The monster's composure, such as it was, broke. "You!" he yelled, looking straight at Jason, "What's your fucking problem! Where's my fucking food?" Then, addressing his captive audience, "This idiot can't get it right!" His lapdog salivated and antiphonally egged him on, adding "yeah" between outbursts. Everybody else was silent, the moment of reckoning had arrived. Jason glared into the monster's eyes with hate tempered by fear. He was expecting him to lunge across the counter at any instant. Somewhere deep down Jason was also experiencing a contradictory impulse, an effervescence of laughter struggling to escape at the foolish clown screaming at him. It was restrained.

Right then Tony said, "Here's your order." The bag was in his hand. Tattoo grabbed it and pushed his way through to the door, dramatically triumphant. As he opened the door he turned around defiantly and glowered one last time. With the pip-squeak sniggering in support he declaimed, "I'll kick his fucking ass," as they both passed through the door. In their absence a vacuum was created by the malignant atmosphere they took with them. Jason giggled nervously and looked at Tony. With his characteristic tranquility he said, "Don't worry about it," and then with contempt in his voice, "Yeah, he gets all badass when he leaves." They both laughed. The customers all deflated a little with sighs of relief. Khaled and Saleem went outside to smoke cigarettes. The phone rang, the cooks turned back to their jobs, equilibrium returned. When things got quieter they would pull out the backgammon board and play a few games.

A Project for Open City
by Cindy Stefans

"...and then she speeds
through a tunnel to a drum
solo until she comes out the
other side, and then she's at
a desk, in an office, and
there's a big sign suspended
above her that says media
slut, and another one that
says more, and she starts
phoning people she doesn't

know and asking them if they
still love her and some of
them say yes..."
(Saroyan, p.125)

42

A Selection Process

Charlie Smith

...under unrivaled fresh weather, each day random variations,
assurances come, studious, revised sensibility occupies itself.
I walk around, notice the impeccable configurations,
    distortions the breeze replaces itself with
in the large philodendron-like trees, massive
spills of wind, a sort of alternating current
    of air streaming above my head. When I am walking
tortured by my disgusting life sometimes
I stop in the middle of an ocean of wind
    and begin to make swimming motions or I watch
the patterns the dying sun makes with the big oleanders the
shadows placed artfully against the high school
    even doves balanced on an electrical wire can be seen
silhouetted in this arrangement. An old woman carrying groceries
passes on my right, moves her lips slightly but doesn't speak.
    Soon, before anyone notices, all this will be gone.
So many claim they lie awake wishing for a new
design, better implants. Yesterday a woman in wind-whipped clothes
    led her child on bikes around the corner, admonishing her
to keep pedaling, but the child sped along
I could see in her eyes
    her power, the child's power; a distant
line of palms, like fiends in the mind, began to wave.
How close we come, I think, to a life very different from this one.

Agents of the Moving Company

Charlie Smith

Rain: morning wadded in a corner, thickening
above the trees' new versions. Still the same early morning walkers,
dogs trotting along under umbrellas, servicemen slapping themselves
    awake
and representatives of the oil company or plumbers in dark blue
    uniforms
approaching pipes. I think about friends who keep diaries,
and those whose lives are impossible to take, how hard It is to live
    with dignity.
retain a sense of life as renewing itself, grace. When I failed
I wanted friends to join me, give up ambition, step back. I drank
for years, finally changed my mind and started over then years later
failed again. No drinks now but the same envy mixed with shame,
still the same familiar unhappy laughter I recognize, from
others fallen short: —one friend goes bitterly on about
his lack of success, drifts to the hors d'oeuvres and stands there
waiting for fortune to find him. I continue my calculations,
think of changing my name, heading off in a slightly different direction.
I sense the querulousness of age, the disappointments
converted into a reactionary philosophy hard to take
by any but the deranged, the petrific glare
maintained through changes in weather, love's ministrations (the dumb
staring, the blanks) ineffective.
You can make a list of what's enviable: form, religion,
family, pension checks like handkerchiefs drying on a mirror,
friends, a sense of fun. I know a man who knows everything about
    basketball.
Another dabbles in computers, exchanges e-letters

with women whose dead husbands were shits. (Stand in the rain if
    you like, pointing
everyone's failure out.) One day my next-door neighbor
wheeled from her house went fluttering in nightclothes through the
    park.
Someone not the city a relative I think came for her,
she's not been heard from since. I know it doesn't matter,
when you break down, if the cabinets and the crockery talk to you
or if you talk back arguing a point of courtesy. Eventually we hope only
for freedom from terror, that the conversation might die out into a
    genial (or slightly quizzical)
gaze held steady for a while then fading like sunlight sinking among
    the nasturtiums.

Evasive Action

Charlie Smith

The clipped possessive moment, the barber on his porch
cutting his son's hair who looks for a second straight into the sun
and then back at his son's head now a golden, nodulous remnant,
a flower if he likes or Lenin's bumpy skull; he puts his scissors down
and goes inside and apologizes to his wife who doesn't understand,
but who accepts his words like a private harvest she's storing up;
and then the son, who's going into the army, comes in, half cut,
and sees them and thinks he understands years of argument,
but doesn't; and goes on to the battlefield where he writes his sister
saying we are not far from the truth of things. watching beyond his hand
two scorpions pick at each other; and thinks of days by the river, of his
father recovering from cancer, singing a song his grandmother
    memorized in Germany,
and his father, who hated his own mother, cursing her, revoking the song;
and the next moment he's blown apart and then sent home in a
    metal coffin
and the parents and the sister get up early on the day of his funeral
and eat breakfast silently on the porch, and this is going on barber
    after barber...

Looking Out

Margaret Park Bridges

I OWN 47 PAIRS OF SUNGLASSES. I DIDN'T START OUT COLLECTING them, I just, whenever I see some I like, I have to have them. Some I buy, some I borrow, some I steal. I don't know, sometimes it's like I'm out of control.

My mom says it's stupid. She says it's always raining and misty in Portland, anyway, what do I need with so many sunglasses? My dad laughs. He says he used to collect bottle caps. At least sunglasses are useful. I mean, I wear them all the time—at school, driving, at the dinner table, even at movies. My mom says she's forgotten what color my eyes are.

But I don't care. I love watching people and knowing they can't tell where I'm looking.

I'm pretty popular at school I guess, but it doesn't matter to me if I am or not, which is probably why I am. I sometimes hang around with a bunch of girls, or rather, they hang around with me. But they're either the kind that are always checking themselves out in the bathroom mirror or else standing around agreeing with everything I say. It's really sad. I generally end up hanging out by myself. If I had to choose, though, I guess I'd stay with the stuck-up girls. At least they don't stand there waiting for you to tell them what to do with their lives.

I'm 16 and I had sex for the first time two years and three months ago. I just wanted to get it out of the way. "Just do it," those commercials kept saying in my head. Thank god the guy didn't want to talk. All he said was, "Want to?" and I said, "Might as well."

Since then I've done it pretty many times, enough that I stopped counting, anyway. Really, I don't know what the big deal is. When

I'm not figuring out the technical details, I'm usually thinking about other things. Like what I'm going to write my history paper on. Or what's for lunch at the cafeteria. The closer a guy gets to me, the farther away I feel. It's funny—a guy can be two inches from my face and inside I'll be like, what am I going to wear to school tomorrow?

Vince is one of the only guys I haven't slept with and he's my boy-friend. Well, I think he is. Really, I don't know what he is, the guy's so strange. He's a man, 36, and it freaks my friends out that he's 20 years older than me. He doesn't seem like it, though. I mean, he still doesn't even have a driver's license. He's probably the only person under 70 in Portland who takes buses or the MAX to get around. It's different now with me, though, since I use my parents' old VW bug—it's older than me, but younger than Vince, and still runs great. So I drive him places. He doesn't like to ask me, I know, but I can tell he's glad. Sometimes I think that's all he likes me for, but then other times he's so quiet I think he doesn't like me at all.

Vince works at a porno movie theater in the projection room. When I call it an erection room he almost smiles. My parents don't know about him, I'm sure they wouldn't like him. I met him at the public library downtown a few weeks ago when I was researching a paper. He was reading a book. I had on my favorite shades—cheap white plastic, cat-eye shaped, with one orange stripe over the left eyebrow—and I could see him glancing over at me, not knowing I was watching him watching me. Even through the shades I could see his dark eyes darting back and forth like mice in a shoebox, and I knew then that he would be my boyfriend, even if he never liked me.

What I like about Vince is I never really know what he's think-ing. He'll tell me if I ask him, sometimes, but it has to be more multiple choice than an essay question. He won't just volunteer information. I know there are things inside, him, though, that've never seen the light of day. It makes me want to keep at him, hoping someday something will seep out.

Sometimes Vince stares at my boobs. I don't really blame him—everybody does. I've got big boobs—too big really—and my mom hates it. I inherited them from her but she had an operation so now she's smaller and naturally she thinks I should be, too. But I like my body the way it is. Guys do, of course. Sure, I slump a little—you would too if you carried two feedbags around every day. Sometimes I can't believe it's actually my own body, like when I look in the mirror. My face doesn't look like someone's who would have two watermelons hanging from it. That's how it feels sometimes. I look like one of those women in Penthouse or something, but inside I'm just...me. It's funny how people look at me though—men I'm talking to staring me straight in the chest, women whispering catty things, I know, about what a slut I am. Like I had some choice in picking my figure. Well, I didn't. As my history teacher once said, "Some just have greatness thrust upon them." I mean, it's just my body. It's not me.

So Vince stares too, but he doesn't say anything. And he doesn't touch. Sometimes his hands seem frozen at his sides, like a rookie bomb squad member who's suddenly terrified of me blowing up in his face. It makes me laugh.

Vince doesn't say much about anything, really. Sometimes I wonder if this is because he has so much going on in his head it's all backed up and can't get out. Or maybe it's really as empty as a handball court with a ball slapping off the walls.

The only time I ever see Vince get excited is when he's watching Jeopardy on TV.

"Richard the Third!" he screams. "What is Richard the Third, not Hamlet, you idiot! Christ."

I love watching him watch, he gets so, like, out of control for once. He isn't thinking about anything else. It's scary. I wish I could watch with him, but I'm too stupid. I can't answer those questions, I never even turned on that show before Vince. Sometimes it bothers me that he's so much smarter than me—he reads everything, that's all he ever really does, is read—but then I think, who cares? I know things he doesn't—like sex. But really inside I feel sad and droopy, like the low part of a hammock. And then I watch him yelling at the TV and this big smile sneaks back onto my face, because even if he doesn't care that much about me, I know he doesn't care if I'm stupid, either.

Reading. That's how come Vince took that job at the porno theater, so he could have time to read while he worked, not because he's a pervert or anything. Which, maybe he is inside, I don't really know, but it sure doesn't seem like it. I swear, there'll be some heavy-duty sex scenes going on all night in front of him and he won't even lift his nose out of *Jude the Obscure*. That's what he was reading when I first met him. I think that was the title. I remember because I kept thinking that's him: Vince the Obscure. He reads like he watches Jeopardy, only quieter. That's how he gets all those answers, he reads like a book a day. I think *War and Peace* took three. I've known him for 23 books. I wonder sometimes how he can move his eyes that fast. I'd be afraid I'd have to get real glasses, then I wouldn't be able to wear all my shades.

So that's about all Vince does: read, watch Jeopardy, and switch reels at Cinema X. And now, he lets me kiss him, though not when he's doing those other things. I have to catch him in between. Then, he usually blushes so I know he likes it, but he won't talk.

"Am I bugging you?" I smile into his mouth, pulling my lips away.

"No . . ." He thrusts his fists into the pockets of his jeans.

"Do you mind if I kiss you, Vince?"

"No."

"No, what?"

"No . . . I don't."

"Am I the first girl you ever kissed?"

He punches his fists deeper like he's digging a hole to China. His pants ride low on his narrow hips.

"Vince? Am I?"

"I don't know."

"You don't know if you ever kissed another girl before? Was it a long time ago? Before I was born?" I like teasing him.

I can see him pulling his face in like sleeves turned inside out, and his adam's apple looks like an acorn I once saw a snake swallow whole. I kiss him again. His lips give a little. I put my palms on his back pockets and pull him near me. I feel him pressing against me, rising like a breadstick in the oven, but he still won't even put his arms around me. This makes me want him even more.

I push him onto the old, threadbare, plaid sofa in his apartment and lie on top of him. He doesn't fight. I'm acting like I know what I'm doing because I've done this with so many other guys, but really inside I'm shaking like my mom's old washing machine. I don't know why. I'm pretty small, only about 106 pounds, and Vince's tall so I know I'm not squashing him, but still he lies there stiff as a board with a nail sticking up.

I kiss him again, on the neck so I can feel his stubble and breathe in his skin. He reaches back behind his head and grabs the remote control. His T-shirt rises, showing a fuzzy median strip up his belly. He turns on the TV and Oprah comes on. I know I'm not going to get anywhere with Vince because he starts watching it and I know he hates that show—he never watches it but now he is.

"Can I get you something to eat?" I ask, sitting up.

"Sure."

"Do you have any food now?"

"Ummm . . . I don't know."

I go into his kitchen and look in the refrigerator. "There's a jar of sauerkraut," I call. "And some old spaghetti sauce with mold on it."

"Okay," he says.

"Want a beer? I brought one of my dad's six-packs, remember? I'll split one with you."

"Okay."

So I open a Henry's and put the bottle to my lips. Maybe I'm the pervert, I think, as the foam runs up and over the rim of the bottle when I pull it away. When Vince puts it to his mouth I feel like he's kissing me for the first time.

At school sometimes I miss Vince so much I can't think of anything else. I feel like one of those kid's dolls that you push a button on the bottom and it falls apart. I told Vince I was going to drop out of school last week so I could spend all my time with him. I didn't mean it. I guess I just wanted to hear him say he'd love that, or even tell me no, I shouldn't, that education is important and that I should worry about my future. But he didn't. He's never said that many words in a row. He just said, "Okay."

Vince works most nights, even on weekends, so the only time we can go out is from three to seven P.M., between the end of school and his first showing. Sometimes I drive us to the Broiler and we get greasy burgers and I have a fresh blackberry shake, but too many of my friends hang out there so we've been going to Rose's instead. It's kind of an institution in Portland. The food's not really as good as people think it is, they just give you huge portions to make up for it. The waitresses are middle-aged Jewish women in gold aprons with little paper crowns nested in their hair and names like Mae, June, Flo, Babs. They call me "honey," and "dear," and say I better not have the corned beef today, it's a little fatty. They tell me to get the chopped liver and I do because, even though I hate it, they look a little like my mother.

So one day I drive us to Rose's and he buys me one of their world-famous cinnamon rolls, which are world-famous not so much for being delicious but for being the size of a curled-up cat. I like to start at the outer edge and unwind it like a spool of thread. It takes a while but it's worth it. The center's the best part.

"You went to college, right, Vince?" I ask.

"Mmhm," he says, wiping mustard off his mouth with his hand. Then, under the table he slides it along his thigh.

"Where'd you go?"

"Dartmouth."

I'm pretty sure this is a good school, but he says it like it's just Portland State.

"Did you like it?"

"I don't know."

"What was it like?"

"I don't know."

"What'd you major in?"

"English."

This doesn't surprise me since I assume he's read every book written in the English language.

"Do you think I should go? To college, I mean?"

"I don't know."

"My mom went to college, but not my dad. He doesn't care but sometimes she acts like it was a big mistake to marry him. She's like, embarrassed of him, sometimes. You know?"

Vince bites into a huge dill pickle.

"Sometimes she acts like she's too good for us," I continue. Vince nods without looking up. "Me and Dad. She's been pushing for me to go to college though we don't hardly have enough money. That's my dad's fault, she says, he didn't go to college so he can't make enough money to send me. 'Parents shouldn't

52

penalize their children for their own inadequacies,' she's always say-ing to him, sometimes in front of me, like I can't hear. Or like I can't understand those words. I can understand."

Vince dips a potato chip in his Coke and crunches it.

"Do you think I'm stupid, Vince?" I ask, eyebrows pinched, obvi-ous as hell I'm fishing for compliments, or even just a reaction.

"I don't know," he says automatically. Then, suddenly, he looks at me real hard, like he can see through my sunglasses into my eyes and even deeper, and my heart flops over like a row of domi-noes. "No," he says, and I believe him.

"What did you do after school today?" my mom asks me later at the dinner table. I'm not eating much of her chicken—"coco van," she corrects me—and my dad is eating it like he eats everything, without chewing hardly, without looking up.

"I hung out with some friends." I've gotten pretty good at lying, but she's gotten pretty good at figuring it out.

"What friends, honey?"

I can tell she adds that "honey" to sweeten the sour look on her face, but I don't give in.

"Oh, just some guys."

"Boys?"

"Oh, boys, girls—the usual suspects."

I glance at my dad and he's licking his fingers, smirking.

"Can't you wait for the rest of us, Ken?" my mom interrupts herself, noticing his empty plate. "Honestly."

"Sorry, Livy," he says, reaching for more rice.

"Well, who are these 'suspects'?" says my mom.

"I don't know, Mom. Just kids. We hang out."

"But, what do you do? What do you talk about? I'd like to hear. Do you know their families? How much do you know about these kids?"

"How much does anybody really know about anybody else?" I say.

My mom looks puzzled, then frustrated, then mad. "Ken…" she sighs.

My dad puts his fork down. "Your mother feels—and so do I—that you should spend more time at home." He eyes my mom, his words coming out like a horse backing out of its stall. "Your mother feels—uh, I mean we feel—that we should spend some more time together…as a family. That we should…get to know each other better."

Please. I'm 16. I need to get to know my parents better like I need a frontal lobotomy. My mom's been watching too much Oprah, I know. That's what happens when you're stuck at home all day—you start thinking if you don't talk to your teenage daughter she'll become a drug addict, a suicide attempter, a victim of autoerotic asphyxiation, a compulsive neatnik, a serial murderer, an old maid, a computer nerd, a porno star, a charge-a-holic, a bed wetter. Scandal of the week. You forget that nobody's ever really normal, and trying to cure them all is like trying to drink from a waterfall. I figure, you might as well stand right under it—you're going to get wet anyway.

So my mom gets out the Monopoly board after dinner and makes us sit down around it on the rug. She makes a bowl of pop-corn and turns off the TV we always keep on for background noise. Suddenly the house feels too quiet, like it's listening to everything too closely. Like what we say better be smart, better be important, because the sound will go echoing through all the rooms like a loudspeaker.

My mom makes us hot chocolate—which my dad hates and which I later see him secretly dumping down the sink and refilling his cup with coffee—and puts marshmallows in mine and hers. I remember laughing when I was little at Mom thinking hot choco-late could cure anything, especially if it had marshmallows floating on top of it. Now she dumps those mini-marshmallows in like they're life rafts for the Titanic.

So my dad takes the hat, my mom takes the dog, and I choose the car, which I know pisses my mom off for some reason, like she thinks it's a sign of something I'm not telling her.

After a while I land on Park Place.

"Aren't you going to buy it?" asks my mom.

"I don't think so," I say. "I'd rather have the cash."

"Well, that's just stupid," says my mom quickly, then, "I mean, you should. It's a good property."

"Why?"

"Because, it is. It's worth a lot. It's a good opportunity for you."

"I thought we were playing against each other, Mom. You should be glad I'm not buying it."

"I'm not playing against you, dear, I'm playing with you. And I just think it would be a big mistake to pass up Park Place. Don't you think it would be, Ken?"

"It's just a game, Liv. Let her buy what she wants."

My mom's eyes look at him all narrow and silvery, her nostrils flaring.

"If you pass this up now," she says to me slowly, "you may never get a second chance."

"I don't care."

I know this is the worst thing I could possibly say to my mom. To her, not caring is worse than disagreeing, I guess because no opinion equals no brain.

"You'll care later!" shouts my mom suddenly, and my dad drops a piece of popcorn. "Wait till your father or I land on it and put up houses and hotels and then you land on it and go bankrupt paying up rent!"

"Oh, I'd never do that to you, honey," my dad says, trying to smile at me.

"But you'd have to, Ken. That's the way it works. You can't just go around making up your own rules."

"It's your roll, Mom."

"Are you buying that property?" Her eyes shimmer like ice cubes.

"No."

"Then I'm buying it for you."

She takes a pile of her own money and puts it in the bank. Then she flips through the cards and gives me the one for Park Place.

"I'm not taking it, Mom," I say, shaking my head. "You can't make me. Take your money back."

"It's free, for god's sake. Take it!" And she flips the card in my face.

"There's no fucking way I'm taking that card, Mom!"

"Take it, you little whore!" she shouts.

I stand up suddenly, knocking over my hot chocolate on the rug. My mom gasps, bringing her palm to her mouth like she can still hold the word in, and I storm out of the silent room, leaving a brown stain that she'll never be able to scrub out.

Suddenly I'm gone. I'm gone and driving fast with all the windows open and the radio blasting and my eyes so fat and blurry I can hardly see through my sunglasses at all.

In a while I find myself down at Vince's apartment and I see him sitting across the street in the coffee shop. I forget that he has Monday nights off. I look in the window and see he's reading an old dog-eared copy of *Lolita*, which I've heard of—something about a young girl who's a nympho. I walk over and sit across from him.

Vince lifts his head. It's I think the first time I've ever seen him look surprised.

"Hi," I say.

"Hi."

"Good chili?" He shoves it toward me but I shake my head. "My mom called me a whore."

Vince stops eating, his mouth full of chili, and looks at me. Then he swallows hard.

"She always says I attract the wrong kind of guys. The kind who 'only want one thing.'" I smile, looking down at my boobs. "Well, only two things, really." I laugh, but my eyes water up and I rub them from under my shades.

Vince takes my hand and my tears seep into his palm. It's the first time he's ever touched me on his own. He stands up, and I let him lead me outside like a little puppy. My fingers weave themselves in his. We cross the street and go upstairs to his apartment. The stairs creak. Inside, the room smells damp and cold from the wind coming through the open windows. I sit on the sofa and watch Vince. He goes into the bathroom without saying anything and turns on the shower.

I go to turn on the TV and see some papers on top of it. I look back at the bathroom door and it's closed so I pick them up. The one on top is a letter to Vince, from some kind of publisher or something. It says, "Congratulations. We are pleased to accept your poem for publication."

The other page has a poem typed on it. It's short and I read it so quickly I have to read it over again twice to actually see what it says. I knew Vince read all the time but I never knew he wrote any-thing, and I feel like a thief breaking into his brain and stealing his thoughts. I just can't turn away, though. I have to look.

At first I think I must be dense because I don't understand it, like most poems I've read. Then something clicks and I see the words clear as day:

Drowning

You thought you had learned to swim
you thought you couldn't drown
then she pulled you under
like a strong current
like electricity
standing your hairs on end
rippling across your skin
wringing your heart out like a sponge.
When she touched your shoulder
by accident you dropped
your book you couldn't hold up
your head your eyelids fell
you sighed with lungs like two stones
you gave up
and sank into deep water.

My heart is beating against my chest like a rainstorm, like the shower in the other room. Suddenly I realize the shower has stopped and Vince is standing in the doorway, still dressed, watching me.

I whip the papers behind my back like some move from a bad old comedy. Vince walks over slowly, reaches around me, and takes my hand.

"I was just...I was looking around and just..." I begin lamely. But Vince only puts the papers back on the TV and cups my one hand in both of his, gently, like a wounded bird.

He wipes a wet streak from my cheek and I understand suddenly that he left the poem there, in the open, on purpose. I look up at him, and for the first time his eyes are all glassy, like mirrors. I can see myself in them, even through my shades. And though he can't see mine, I know he can tell how I'm feeling, too. I kiss his calloused palm, then he slowly runs his fingers down my neck, across my chest, and looks at me like I'm the most fragile, amazing thing he's ever seen. My heart thuds like a bass guitar in his hands.

Vince leads me into his bedroom. The curtains flutter. The sheets feel all cool and damp as he lays me down. Then he leans forward to kiss me.

"Wait," I say, and I take off my sunglasses and drop them on the floor.

"He came in at a time when people could get despicable. A need for immediate gratification pushed their baseness to the surface. This impatience made for embarassing displays, unpleasant demonstrations of humankind at its pettiest. It was almost a war. They wanted their lunch served with alacrity and if it wasn't, overwrought responses were often unleashed —from yelling and screeching to pleading and threatening. All for some inauthentic serviceable Mexican food made in nearly fast-food time."

(Weyland, p.27)

Pearl River Delta, China

Harvard Project on the City

The Harvard Project on the City examines the effects of modernization on the contemporary city by focusing on the most intense yet vaguely understood processes of urbanization. Its research identifies those forces which perceptively alter the spatial and temporal character of the city, yet defy confinement within the existing descriptive framework of the disciplines of architecture, landscape architecture, and urban planning. In its first year the Project studied the Pearl River Delta region in southern China, a conglomeration of cities that produces approximately 500 square kilometers of built substance a year, manifesting in unprecedented and mutant urban conditions. The following terms are part of a larger vocabulary formulated to reveal and identify the significance of forces, phenomena, and processes of urbanization previously shrouded by incomprehension.

The Project is conducted by Rem Koolhaas and thesis students at the Harvard University Graduate School of Design. The participants in the first year of the Project were: Bernard Chang, Mihai Craciun, Nancy Lin, Yuyang Liu, Katherine Orff, Stephanie Smith, with Marcela Cortina and Jun Takahashi.

廣州市
Guangzhou

惠州市
Huizhou

東江 Dong

石龍鎮
Shilongzhen

東莞市
Dongguan

番禺
Panyu

順德
Shunde

虎門
Humen

太平
Taiping

黃埔
Huangpu

PEARL RIVER DELTA

莘沙
Shasha

深圳市
Shenzhen

寶安
Baoan

黃田機場
深圳機場
Shenzhen Airport

羅湖
Lo Wu

蛇口
Shekou

中山
Zhongshan

珠江口
Zhu Jiang Mouth

福田
Futian

元朗
Yuen Long

江門市

屯門
Tuen Mun

珠海
Zhuhai

大嶼山
Lantau Island

九龍
Kowloon

香港
Hong Kong

澳門
Macau

CITY OF EXACERBATED DIFFERENCE© (COED©)

The traditional city strives for a condition of balance, harmony and a degree of homogeneity. The CITY OF EXACERBATED DIFFERENCE©, on the contrary, is based on the greatest possible difference between its parts — complementary or competitive. In a climate of permanent strategic panic, what counts for the CITY OF EXACERBATED DIFFERENCE© is not the methodical creation of the ideal, but the opportunistic exploitation of flukes, accidents and imperfections. Though the model of the CITY OF EXACERBATED DIFFERENCE© appears brutal — to depend on the robustness and primitiveness of its parts — the paradox is that it is, in fact, delicate and sensitive. The slightest modification of any detail requires the readjustment of the whole to reassert the equilibrium of complementary extremes.

INFRASTRUCTURE© Infrastructures, which were mutually reinforcing and totalizing, are becoming more and more competitive and local; they no longer pretend to create functioning wholes but have become instruments of secession. Instead of network and organism, INFRASTRUCTURE© now creates enclave and impasse; no longer the "*grand recit*" but the parasitic swerve. Malfunctioning is also a form of functioning. Each INFRASTRUCTURE© has both a positive and a negative program. It enables *and* prevents.

SCAPE© PRD. An (exploded) mountain, a skyscraper, and a ricefield in every direction, nothing between excessive height and the lowness of a continuous agricultural/light industrial crust; between the *lofty* and the loft. SCAPE©, neither city nor landscape, is the new post-urban condition: it will be the arena for a terminal confrontation between architecture and landscape. It can only be understood as an apotheosis of the PICTURESQUE©.*

*PICTURESQUE© Revenge of the anti-idealistic. A mode of making and perceiving space, invented by Chinese gardeners in the 16th century, which insists on the juxtapositions and relationships between objects, rather than their singular presence.

INFRARED© Driven underground by the forces of global economy, the Chinese Communist Party safeguards its totalitarian ideology by moving into the invisible spectrum of politics. INFRARED© is a covert strategy of compromise and double standard, a preemptory reversal of history that links nineteenth-century idealism with the realities of the twenty-first-century.

CONCESSION© Yielding as tactic. Traditionally China has used the PRD to make CONCESSIONS©: Hong Kong and Macau were ceded to Britain and Portugal as receptacles for controlled importation of Westernness, allowing the rest of China to remain "pure." In a similar way, Special Economic Zones are CONCESSIONS©: land sacrificed for free-market experiments.

老东门商城

MARKET REALISM© Is there a connection between China's recent communist history and its present idolatry of the Market? Socialist Realism is the Stalinist doctrine that suggests that art should depict, in the most realistic way, a final condition of realized Utopia, rather than dwell on the imperfections of the present, or the sacrifices on the road toward its implementation. It is a brilliant formula for desire simultaneously deferred and consummated. The present interval between Market promise and Market delivery is explained by MARKET REALISM©, a speculative fervor that does not demand instant gratification in the form of profit, rentability, or a real relationship between *supply* and *demand* — the first overwhelming, the second still defined by ORACULAR MAGIC©.* Socialist Realism: MARKET REALISM© = toil: speculation.

*ORACULAR MAGIC© Seemingly random, essentially unpredictable nature of the market 'goals' and 'deals' that depends on an amalgamation of Confucian and Communist tradition, produces... now operative in a new market-based context as the foundation of MARKET REALISM©.

CHINESE ARCHITECT© The most important, influential, and powerful architect on earth. The average lifetime construction volume of the CHINESE ARCHITECT© in housing alone is greater than thirty 30-story high-rise buildings. The CHINESE ARCHITECT© designs the largest volume in the shortest time for the lowest fee. There are 1/10 the number of architects in China than there are in the U.S., each of whom designs 5 times the project volume in 1/5 the time, while earning 1/10 the design fee. This implies an efficiency of 2,500 times that of an American architect.

Architects as a percentage of total national population.

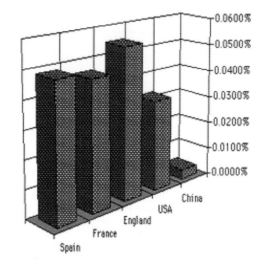

There are 1/10 the number of architects in China than in the US . . .

Design fee schedule as a percentage of total construction cost.

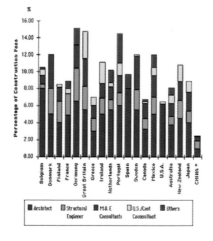

. . . earning 1/10 the design fee . . .

million m2

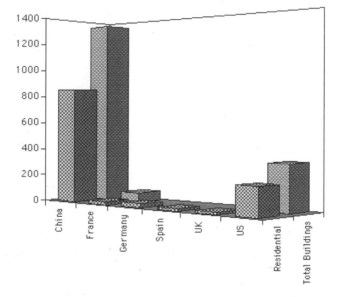

1992 Total
building
construc-
tion by
floor area.

. . . yet designing 5 times the project volume.

"Elmo once called his mother to her face a boo-hooer. That epithet rankled in her heart for a long time."
(Purdy, p.145)

Photo by Courtney Lasseter

What They Did

David Means

WHAT THEY DID WAS COVER THE STREAM WITH LONG SLABS OF reinforced concrete, the kind with steel rods through it. Maybe they started with a web of rods, then concrete poured over, making a sandwich of cement and steel. Perhaps you'd call it more of a creek than a stream, or in some places, depending on the vernacular, a narrow gorge through that land, a kind of small canyon with steep sides. They covered the cement slabs with a few feet of fill, odds and ends, cement chunks, scraps, bits of stump and crap from excavating the foundation to the house on the lot, which was about fifty yards in front of the stream. Then they covered the scraps and crap with a half foot of sandy dirt excavated near Lake Michigan, bad topsoil, the kind of stuff that wiped out the Okies in the dust bowl storms. Over that stuff they put a quarter foot of good topsoil, rich dank humus that costs a bundle, and then over that they put the turf, rolled it out the way you'd roll out sheets of toilet paper; then they watered the hell out of it and let it grow together while the house, being finished, was sided and prepped for the first walkthroughs by potential owners. His nesting instinct, he explained, shaking hands with Ingersol, the real estate guy. Marjorie Howard rested the flat of her hand on her extended belly and thought due in two weeks but didn't say it. A few stray rocks, or boulders, were piled near the edge of the driveway and left there as a reminder of something, maybe the fact that once this had been a natural little glen with poplars and a few white birch and an easy slope down to the edge, the drop-off to the creek or brook or whatever it is now hidden under slabs of concrete—already sinking slightly but not noticeable to the building inspector who has no idea that the creek is there because it's one of those out of sight out of mind things, better left unsaid so as not to worry the future owners who might worry, if that's their nature, over a creek under reinforced concrete. So all one might see from the kitchen, a big one with the little cooking island in the middle with burners and the wide window, is a slope down to the very end of the yard where a tall cedar fence is being installed, a gentle slope with a very slight sag in the center—but no hint, not in the least, of any kind of stream running through there. In the trial the landscaper guys—or whatever they are—called it a creek, connoting something small and supposedly lessening the stupidity of what they did. The DA called it a river, likened it to River Styx, or the Phlegethon, the boiling river of blood, not citing Dante or anything but just using the words to the befuddlement of the jury, four white men and three white women, three black women, two male Hispanics. Slabs were placed over the creek, or river, whatever, on both adjacent lots, too, same deal, bad soil, humus, rolled turf, sprinkled to high hell until it grew together but still had that slightly fake look that that kind of grass has years and years after the initial unrolling, not a hint of chokeweed or bramble or crabgrass to give it a natural texture. And the river turned to the left further up, into the wasted fields and wooded area slated for development soon but held off by a recession (mainly in heavy industry), pegs with slim fluorescent orange tape fluttering the wind, demarcating future "estates" and cul-de-sacs and gated communities once the poplars and white birch on that section were scalped down to the muddy tire-track ruts. What they did was cover another creek up elsewhere in the same manner, and in doing so they noticed that the slabs buckled slightly upward for some reason, the drying constriction of concrete on the steel rods; and therefore, to counterweight, they hung small galvanized garden buckets of cement down from the centers of each slab on short chains, a bucket per slab that allowed a slight downward pucker until the hardening—not drying, an engineer explained in the trial, but setting, a chemical change, molecules rearranging and so on and so forth—evened it out. So when the rescue guy went down twelve feet sashaying the beam of his miner's lamp around, he saw a strange sight, hardly registered it but saw it, a series of dangling buckets fading out into the darkness above the stream until the creek turned slightly towards the north and disappeared in shadow. What they could've done instead, the engineer said, was to divert the stream to the north (of course costing big bucks and also involving impinging on a railroad right-of-way owned by Conrail, or Penn Central), a process that involves trenching out a path, diverting the water, and allowing the flow to naturally erode out a new bed. What they could've done, a different guy said, an environmental architect who turned bright pink when he called himself that, ashamed as he was of tooting his own horn with the self-righteousness of his title—or so it seemed to Mr. Howard, who of the two was the only one able to compose himself enough to bring his eyes forward. Mrs. Howard dabbled her nose with a shredded Kleenex, sniffed, caught tears, sobbed, did what she had to do. She didn't attend all of the trial, avoiding the part when the photos of the body were shown. She avoided the diagrams of the stream and lot, the charts and cutaways, cross sections of the slabs. Nor could she stand the sight of the backyard, the gaping hole, the yellow police tape and orange cones, and now and then, bright as lightning, a television news light floating there, a final wrap-up for the eleven o'clock, even CNN coming back days later for a last taste of it. What they could have done is just leave the stream where it was and buffer it up along the sides with a nice-looking, cut-stone retaining wall because according to one expert, the creek, a tributary into the Kalamazoo River, fed mainly by run-off from a local golf course and woods, was drying up slowly anyhow. In the next hundred years or so it would be mostly gone, the guy said, not wanting to contradict the fact that it might have been strong enough to erode the edges of the slab support and pull it away or something, no one was sure, to weaken it enough for the pucker to form. The pucker is what they called it. Not a hole. It's a fucking hole, Mr. Howard said. No one on the defense would admit that it was one of those buckets yanking down in that spot that broke a hole through. Their side of the case was built on erosion, natural forces, an act of God. No one would admit that it had little or nothing to do with the natural forces of erosion. Except silently to himself Ralph Hightower, the site foreman, who came up with the bucket idea in the first place, under great pressure from the guys in Lansing who were funding the project, and his boss, Rob, who was pushing for completion in time for the walkthroughs in spring. Now and then he thought about it, drank a couple of beers and smoked one of his Red Owls and mulled over his guilt the way someone might mull over a very bad ball game, one that lost someone some cash; he didn't like kids a bit, even innocent little girls, but he still felt a small hint of guilt over the rescue guy having to go down there and see her body floating fifteen yards downstream like that and having to wade the shallows in the cramped dark through that spooky water to get her; he'd waded rivers before a couple of times snagging steelhead salmon and knew how slippery it was going over slime-covered rock. Other than Ralph Hightower and his beer, guilt and blame was distributed between ten-odd people until it was a tepid and watered-down thing, like a single droplet of milk in a large tumbler of water—barely visible, a light haze, if even that. All real guilt hung on Marjorie Howard, who saw her girl disappear, vanish, gulped whole by the smooth turf, which was bright green-blue under a clear, absolutely brilliant spring sky. All that rolled turf was just bursting with photosynthetic zest, although you could still tell it was rolled turf by the slightly different gradient hues where the edges met, melded— this after a couple of good years of growth and the sprinkler system going full blast on summer eves and Mr. Howard laying down carefully plotted swaths of Weed & Feed (she'd just read days before her girl vanished in the yard that it was warmth that caused dormant seeds and such to germinate, not light but simply heat). Glancing outside, her point of focus was past the Fisher Price safety gate, which was supposed to mind the deck stairs. She saw Trudy go down them, her half-balanced wobble walk, just able to navigate their awkward width (built way past code which is almost worse than breaking code and making them too narrow or too tall, stupidly wide and short for no good reason except some blunder the deck guy made, an apprentice deck kid, really). She was just about halfway across the yard, just about halfway to the cedar fence, making a beeline after something—real or imagined, who will ever know?—in her mind's eye or real eye, the small bird bath they had out there, perhaps. What they did was frame the reinforcement rods—web or just long straight ones—in wooden rectangles back in the woods, or what had been woods and then was just a rut-filled muddy spot where, in a few months, another house would come. Frames set up, the trucks came in and poured the concrete in and the cement set and then a large rig was brought in to lift the slabs over to the creek, or stream, or whatever, which by this time was no longer the zippy swift-running knife of water but was so full of silt and mud and runoff from the digging it was more of an oozing swath of brown substance. Whatever fish were still there were so befuddled and dazed they'd hardly count as fish. Lifted them up and over, guiding with ropes, and slapped them down across the top of the stream—maybe twenty in all, more or less depending on how large they were. Then more were put down when they moved up to the next lot, approved or not approved by the inspector who never really came around much anyhow. Then the layers of crappy soil stuff and then the humus and then the rolls of turf while the other guys were roofing and putting up the siding, and the interior guys were cranking away slapping drywall up fast as they could with spackling crews coming behind them, then the painters working alongside the carpet crews with nail guns popping like wild, and behind them, or with them, alongside, whatever, the electricians doing finishing fixtures and the furnace and all that stuff in conjunction with the boss's orders, and the prefab window guys, too, those being slapped into preset frames, double-paned, easy-to-clean and all that, all in order to get ready for the walkthroughs the real estate guys, operating out of Detroit, had lined up. Already the demand was so high on account of the company which was setting up a new international headquarters nearby. This was a rather remote setting for such a venture, but on account of low taxes (an industrial park) and fax machines and all the new technology it didn't matter where your headquarters were so long as they were near enough to one of those branch airports and had a helipad on the roof for CEOs' arrivals and departures. Housing was urgently necessary for the new people. The walkthrough date in the spring because the company up-and-running date was July first. What the ground did that day was to open up in a smooth, neat little gape—which wasn't more than thirty pounds, maybe less but enough to spar forces already at bay, but that doesn't matter, the facts, the physics, are nothing magical, as one engineer testified, and if this tragedy hadn't've happened—his words—certainly the river itself would have won out, eroded the edge, caused the whole slab to fall during some outdoor barbecue or something, a whole volleyball or badminton game swallowed up in a big gulp of earth. There one second, gone the next was how someone, best left unsaid who, but most likely CNN, described what Marjorie Howard saw—or sensed, because really the phrase seems like a metaphysical poem or maybe a philosophical precept (bad choices on the part of the contractors, no, not choice, nothing about choice there, or maybe fate of God if that has to do with it, one local news report actually used the phrase Act of God, if it's a phrase). But it was an accurate account because standing in the kitchen it was like that, seeing her go, watching her vanish, and all the disbelief that she had seeing it, the momentary loss of sanity and the rubbing of her eyes in utter, fantastical disbelief, would burgeon outward in big waves and never go away no matter what, so that between that one second she was there and the one where her little girl was gone was a wide opening wound that would never be filled, or maybe finished is the word. What they did was guide the slabs down, doing the whole job in one morning because the crane was slated to be used on a project all the way over in Plainwell, and then think while eating lunch from black lunch tins afterwards, feet up on a stump, Ho Hos and Twinkies at the end, looking at the slabs, the river gone, vanished, the creek gone, vanished, nothing but slabs of still-damp cement swirled with swaths of mud—the buckets hanging beneath them out of view—we did a good morning's work, nothing more, nothing less.

Dead Man Writes*

Rick Moody

Resuscitated man relates vision from beyond.
Dogs howling indicate death.
Flowers bloom when touched.
Incubus comes in sleep and has sex.
Revenants eat.

Non-malevolent ghost haunts scene of former misfortune.
Sham relics perform miracles if faith is great.
Imitation of jumping into fire without injury: dupe burned up.
Land of dead across water.
Resuscitated man relates vision from beyond.

Revenants eat.
Concern of ghost about belongings of its lifetime.
Ghostly bell.
Dogs howling indicate death.
Dead friends come for dying man's soul.
Miraculous healing by saints.

---

*Index entries by Stith Thompson. From his *Motif-Index of Folk-Literature*. Chicago: University of Chicago Press, 1966.

Domesticity*
for Jo Ann Beard

Rick Moody

He had an eye for plaids that was just incredible
Ebony chests inlaid with mother-of-pearl
Dinner—always Thai and always delicious
The feeling throughout is of space stretching into the outdoors
A Portuguese miracle in tile
Sixteen immaculate schemes of box hedge
The door which slides back on metal tracks is classic barn style

What we got from the residents as an opening salvo was that they
    really liked color
I recycle and reaccessorize just by mood or by season—it's in, it's out,
    it's summer, it's winter.
The residence Cole and Fischer purchased had been renovated by a
    previous owner from a modest suburban ranch house
I wanted it to be heavy and volumetric

It is standard operating procedure for many married people. Build a
    vacation house to escape every now and then where—after the
    children are grown and the appeal of city life has waned—you
    can eventually retire
Charles and Shirley Comeau are the heirs of an energetic pioneer
    tradition

If you have a French room, you have to have an Italian piece to
    make it work
The cowgirls in Joyce Larsen's studio are not kitsch at all,
    but images of the way life was once lived by the woman

who collected them
(The fine house he built for himself signified his membership in the
new ruling class)

*Entire contents from *Architectural Digest: The International Magazine of Fine Interior Design*, September 1993.

Immortality*

Rick Moody

yellow is superior, then, successively, black, variegated, and white
tastes ambrosial
I asked the boss about the history of puppy meat
popular in people's daily life since recent years in accordance with
    increasing living conditions
suffusing an exquisite fragrance all around
Scald puppy with boiling water
Puppy meat is a kind of good nutriment
eat puppy meat in winter, especially on the Winter Solstice
worldwide famous Sichuan pungent chafing dish
By the criteria of the puppy's fur color, the quality of the meat
    is classified into four classes
Like butcher pig, it doesn't need to peel the skin when slaughter puppy
glossy, fresh fatty puppy meat and curling up tails
Use burning iron sheet to burn until the puppy meat appears
    snow white
add nothing but a little alcohol
When you drink mellow puppy kidney wine, you may feel like an
    immortal

---

*Assembled from a translated in-flight magazine article on Chinese cuisine.

Two Sonnets for Stacey*

Rick Moody

They're coming to America. —Neil Diamond

I.
I like mechanics magazines.
I think I would like the work of a librarian.
There seems to be a lump in my throat much of the time.
It would be better if almost all laws were thrown away.
I have not lived the right kind of life.
I like poetry.
I would like to be a florist.
I believe in the second coming of Christ.
I believe in law enforcement.
I am afraid of losing my mind.
Children should be taught all the main facts of sex.
I like to flirt.
I have used alcohol excessively.
I loved my mother.

II.

Sometimes at elections I vote for men about whom I know very little.

I have never been in love with anyone.

Sometimes my voice leaves me or changes even though I have no cold.

Bad words, often terrible words, come into my mind and I cannot get rid of them.

At times I have enjoyed being hurt by someone I loved.

Horses that don't pull should be beaten or kicked.

It is great to be living in these times when so much is going on.

I am a special agent of God.

I have never noticed any blood in my urine.

I think Lincoln was greater than Washington.

I like repairing a door latch.

I sometimes feel that I am about to go to pieces.

I feel like jumping off when I am on a high place.

I like movie love scenes.

CaCO$_2$

A Project for Open City

by Matthew Ritchie

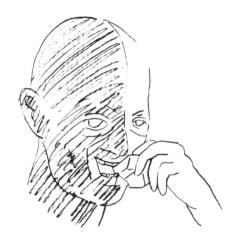

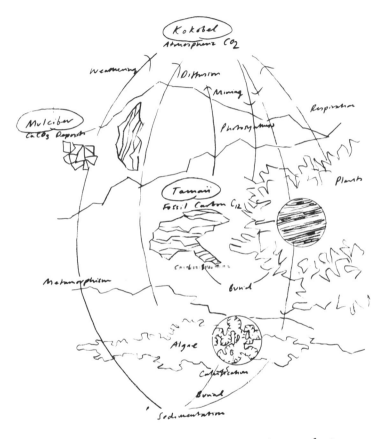

Calcium Carbon Oxygen Cycle

"There can be dozens of categories in a single evening: best wig, best butch queen walking in drag for the first time, best dressed for a night at the Clinton White House. There are even special categories for very short drag queens (midget model's effect), and those who weigh over 180 pounds."

(Cunningham, p.175)

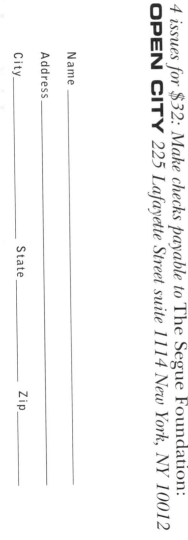

ATE AT NIGHT, A VERY
ding off of it. There's
door, which can be
. But you're opening
yone's inside. You're
, because you're the
with you."

y front terrace, Dan
d loses himself in the
" he's working out to
sits below his feet, a
out here to smoke.
xpensive tin, blowing
ver Haight-Ashbury.
m his huge head of
ously, as he has a way
with old gray matter
-adjusting is a 1960s-
-power, the smile a
but lordly; beautiful,
nken. He seems too
al plummet off the
cohol helps, both of
security geek, has a
I, one bottle at a
time, have conquered a large number of buzzwords.

Harder to fathom is Farmer's claim to geekiness. He wears

thick black leather pants, boots, and a biker jacket over a sawed-off black T-shirt featuring a human skull, humanoid figures, two salmon, and the credo SPAWN TILL YOU DIE; a tiny skull with a ruby eye pierces his left nipple. There's a small golden earring in the corner of his left eyebrow, dog-tags from his days as a U.S. Marine adorn his neck, and handcuffs hang from his studded leather belt: Farmer, as any who've dialed into his confessional homepage (at www.fish.com) can tell you, is a practicing sadist (he prefers the term "top"), equally fascinated with ultra-violence, Zen mysticism, and confessional poetry, openly bisexual, and a ravenous polygamist (he prefers "polyamorous").

"You open Door Seventeen Thousand," he continues. "Lo and behold, there's another door at the end of the room, and you see something happening through that door."

"What do you see?"

"An intruder. Presumably some pain-in-the-ass network cracker. Quite possibly the end of security not only for Office Seventeen Thousand but much or all of your multi-billion-dollar corporation, Swiss bank, your military installation."

"How did he get in there?"

"Simple. Remember I told you about the addresses on the doors? Well, this building we're in now has an address, such-and-such Oak Street. But it's also on the corner of Oak and Ashbury. If you slap an address and a mail-chute on the Ashbury side, convince the postman they're real, then my mail is your mail."

"It's that simple to break into a Swiss bank?"

"Go through a little glass and you're in."

"Or a military installation?"

"Probably easier. C'mon." Farmer hops off the rail. "Let's fire up old Satan."

By the time we get into the second bedroom, Death is already curled and purring like an old familiar on the chair of the Sparc-station, the powerful workstation that serves as Farmer's main computer at home. The $25,000 stack of small off-white boxes, one of three in the apartment, is also named Death.

"Satan is really a much-maligned fellow," Farmer says a bit testily, calling up the program he co-authored and dumped on the Internet almost two years ago. "All he really does is case the joint."

I've been prodding Farmer for days to show me Satan "in action," but he despises the act of network cracking. The logo, a line-drawing of a long-tailed daemon in a trenchcoat, appears on the screen, followed by a target-selection prompt.

"Can we break into NASA?" I ask.

"That's a little problematic."

"Why?"

"I kinda work for them."

"How about the NSA?" Farmer gives me one of his smiles.

"You work for them too?"

"It's a long story," he demurs. "Any branch of the military you're feeling curious about tonight?"

I was reading about stealth bombers this morning.

Farmer types in hq.af.mil., then gives me one of his smiles: See how easy?

In fact, there's nothing more to it: At lightning speed, the screen fills with a list of software the air force is running these days, each vulnerability highlighted by a red dot. Farmer hits a few more keys, and in four seconds we're in, scrolling down a vast directory: memos, e-mail, classified reports and inventories, updates. Even at the speed we're scrolling, I see items referring to stealth bombers.

"That fellow's busy," Farmer points to a sub-directory trailing six figures of characters. "Probably a sysadmin [system administrator], high security clearance. If I wanted the keys to this kingdom, I'd click on him. And,"…he drops an ominous pause. "I'd be committing a very serious felony."

"Have we already committed one?"

Farmer pushes hair away from his eyes as he thinks about it. "I don't know. How do you feel about it?"

I'm not sure. Fairly uneasy, actually, that the only thing keeping me from a crime is my own feeling about its criminality. I also see possibilities. April 15 isn't far off: A little nudge from the Debit column to You Are Owed…? "How secure do you imagine the — Corporation's system is?" I ask (my boss).

"In computer terms, that's a meaningless question. Secure against what?"

"Against me."

Farmer exits the air force, types, and suddenly we're in the bowels of my employer, scrolling down an endless menu. "A simple answer to your question? You can break into anyone."

The doors leading off the long corridor now signify more than a simple gain and loss: These are my colleagues, friends, suspected enemies, years of emotional investment, the future. The unease grows. "Let's get out of here."

Farmer gives me the beautiful, approving smile, like one of Jonathan Swift's Houyhnhnms: innocence born of reason. "Aren't you ever tempted?" I ask.

"Not really," he says. "Don't forget: I'm the security geek."

His business card, from Sun Microsystems Laboratories, identifies him as such: Iconoclast, 2nd Class/Security Research Guy. Accent is on the Research, which carries huge cachet at a braintrust like Sun. It also affords Farmer the opportunity to indulge an almost limitless capacity for sloth. Like most of his generation, he produces in bursts of compulsive labor, then spends months writing E-mail and poems. On rare occasions, he moonlights (at $3000 per day) as a security consultant; once or twice a year, he'll let Sun trot him out at high-tech conferences around the world as a computer-security poster-boy—leather, piercings, handcuffs, and all. More than once, he's found the door barred by guards unwilling to believe he's the guest of honor.

It seems strange on first meeting Farmer—so angelic and harmless—that the security of untold billions rests on the new, little-known field that he, at 34, is now a past master of. The world, like it or not, revolves around software and networks that ease and increase the flow of information, but the pace of development is so rapid, the field so competitive, that little if any thought is given to the vulnerabilities of products by the time they go on sale. For every innovation that connects two people on the Net, a new hole—almost perforce—is opened for hackers (Farmer calls them "crackers") or more serious criminals to waltz into your system. Even if you go online with a fully secure network, holes will eventually open. "It would take a great philosopher to explain why those breakdowns always occur," Farmer says. "In essence, it's the universal law of entropy."

Writing programs (or code) that make life and work easier and fuller takes knowledge, time, and vision; it doesn't take a Ph.D. in programming, however, to subvert that hard work for selfish ends. Anyone with a capacity or a program for breaking passwords, for example, can probably use your program to go pretty much wherever he wants. Once inside, a rudimentary knowledge of ubiquitous software such as Sendmail (which almost every office in the world uses) is all that's needed to cybersail down that long corridor from office to office, copying, deleting, altering, or just leaving nasty messages. The damage done thus far—losses due to theft of secrets, assets, and intellectual property—is, by definition, impossible to calculate. Estimates range from three to fifteen billion dollars annually. It depends who you ask.

Two springs ago, when Farmer announced the release of Satan (Security Administrator Tool for Analyzing Networks) with his collaborator, Weitse Venema, a Javanese researcher at the Netherlands' University of Eindhoven, he sent a chill of insecurity through the computer world. The date it became available, April 5, was simply Farmer's thirty-third birthday, but the timing couldn't have been more perfect: Wall Street riding a bull run that shattered all market wisdom and convention, largely on high-tech stocks understood by very few; some 30 million people online; Madison Avenue heralding the Internet's imminent global community— safe conduit for everything from encrypted gossip to digital cash.

Satan threatened to tear it all down. Tools for probing holes in individual computers had long been available, but they were labor-intensive, expensive, and made by the close-knit security community for its own consumption. Satan, which is essentially a search engine linked to a compendium of all known software, had the ability to instantly scan for the security vulnerabilities of massive networks—corporate, military, institutional—with a single, scattershot glance. And it was idiot-friendly—so long as the idiot had access to and basic knowledge of a Unix-based computer: Downloading takes 5 minutes. The program comes with easy-to-follow instructions. You simply call the site or homepage you want to invade, steal from, deface, or, if you're feeling honorable, learn about, then follow Satan's commands. Satan, like his namesake, doesn't actually take you into that site; like Faust, you have to make that decision independently.

Most ominous-seeming, Satan was free: Farmer and Venema had turned down millions for it, then stood their ground when they were threatened if they went ahead with their free down-loading—to be "sued out of existence," and worse. "Suddenly," prophesied *The New York Times*, "cracking a computer's security won't require special technical skills, but simply the will to do it."

Quotes flew out to the press and over the Net like a computer virus: "Satan is like a gun," said Mike Higgins, chief of the computer-security team at the Department of Defense, "and this is like handing a gun to a twelve-year-old."

"Now the bad guys can pull it down and use your own weapons against you," warned Jim Settle, former head of the FBI's computer crimes squad.

"It's like distributing high-powered rocket launchers through-out the world," said Donn Parker, security analyst for SRI, a Silicon Valley quasi-government think-tank, "free of charge, available at your local library or school, and inviting people to try them out by shooting at somebody."

"...Get ready for an onslaught of people using this tool to attack," read an SRI report Parker co-authored. "It discovers vulner-abilities for which there are no known solutions." The report cautioned sysadmins to install the intruder-alert software known as a TCP/IP wrapper and call in experts to erect or upgrade fire-walls, the network equivalent of a moat, at the company's juncture to the Internet. The irony was immediate to everyone familiar with Satan's makers: In their capacity as consultants, Farmer and Venema are the experts you call to fix your firewalls; Venema invented the TCP/IP wrapper.

"Unfortunately," said Farmer, "this is going to cause some serious damage to some people." It probably didn't help when he acknow-ledged that the network cracker Kevin Mitnick had broken into www.fish.com and downloaded a prototype. It certainly didn't help that he made his sexual proclivities as public as he did Satan. Silicon Graphics, the Silicon Valley corporation where he held the self-assumed title of Network Security Czar, fired him shortly before the release date.

Then something funny happened. Though an estimated ten

thousand Internet accounts sucked up copies, the brave new world didn't miss a beat. Some Satan-driven break-ins were reported (and, doubtless, a good many occurred unreported), but networks and individuals continued to subscribe at a dizzying pace, suspect IPOs and stocks with absurd P/E ratios soared in price and volume, and ads with nuns and peasants kvelling about surfing the global community flooded the same high-end slots. If anything, Farmer's openness and nonprofit downloading seemed to presage a continuing Age of Innocence; at worst, it was a case of old-fashioned exhibitionism tied to a technical issue, one easily solved by other geeks. "I don't care who he's in the hot tub with," said Bill Cheswick, a senior researcher at Bell Labs, "his [programming] code is good."

Farmer was the first to say that the buzz Satan created was unreal. He and Venema inserted a "white paper" ("How to Improve the Security of Your Site by Breaking into It") that heralded the program's true intentions, then added an audio key that set off the Public Enemy song "Don't Believe the Hype," and a "REPENT" command, which changed the Satan command to Santa Claus. Both were cyber-tropes that underscored their true ambition for Satan: to blow the cover of obscurity that computer security has always managed to veil itself with.

Writing the code for Satan took Farmer years of tedious labor. It functions so well because it is a compendium of all known security software and all known vulnerabilities: Whether you're a Swiss bank or a nuclear facility or a hamburger chain, you'll be using software that Satan knows the loopholes of. "All I did," says Farmer, still reveling in the bizarreness of his fifteen par-secs of fame, "was write a program. Overnight, I become a rock star." When he consulted at Geffen Records, employees accustomed to passing Axl Rose or Madonna in the halls came flocking when they heard he was in the building. And women—"the kind you dream about," he says— began e-mailing photos of themselves in bondage, graphically detailing acts of submission they'd be willing to undergo. "This image," Farmer says, "would, of course, burst instantly if these people had any idea how technical and laborious writing code is."

The issues he'd raised—of privacy and freedom, of responsibility and authority, of the increasingly fine line between intelligence and reason—these were, of course, far more complex than the zeros and ones of Satan's code. By harnessing so much "destructive" power, then unleashing it with such benign effect, he'd augured the debate of a future we're moving toward at warp-speed: Who's running this global community anyhow? And this was no nerd posing as agent provocateur, it was a sincere challenge, and it was coming from the vanguard of a paradigm shift that will soon make the cultural changes of the sixties seem like the hula-hoop craze. In a place like Northern California, where Farmer can leave his corporate office, jump on his black Honda Shadow, and step off a half-hour later into the free-for-all of a cross-dressing bondage club—without having to stop home for a change of clothes—that shift has probably already occurred.

It's a bizarre shift. "Take your money and put it in a safe," says Farmer, trying to explain it. "Then put that safe in the bottom of a vault, and rig the vault with mines. Are you secure? No. Someone will find a way in.

"Now take that safe, put it on Main Street, leave the door open, and put full-page ads about the money in the local paper. When you can do that and hold your money, then you're secure."

Farmer was born out here, the son of university people, but grew up in Bloomington, Indiana, where his father taught international economics. He was an unhappy kid, his memories of childhood largely of the books that lined the walls of his house, and of reading: from *Curious George* to *Gigabit Networking*, a path lined with fantasy/sci-fi. He remembers the household as "neither hostile nor affectionate, just sterile," and himself as a lazy, hostile 97-pound weakling with poor eyesight, his interface with the physical world not coming until arcade games went digital: first Pong, then Tank, Space Lords, Asteroids. He liked baseball, but his fascination was for working out percentages and averages on his slide-rule, then the early pocket calculators. He wanted to become an astronaut.

As with many of his caste, college was a wash, both academically and socially: He flew through science and statistics classes at Purdue, but when he learned NASA required 20/20 vision, he drifted down to the pool hall. Celibate and terrified, his first encounter was with a beautiful blond French student, Sheri, whom he saw in the pool hall, playing an amazing game of Space Invaders. He went home with her to meet her lover, a high-school music teacher, and sat on the couch with him while Sheri walked in and out of the room, modeling outfits. When she came out naked, Farmer's mind went into hyperspace, and he couldn't even look at her.

It would be years before he'd work it out. For the moment, he was simply convinced no one wanted him—not his parents, not NASA, not Sheri—which made him angry, aroused, and even angrier. Future colleagues, living out scenarios of disenfranchisement and awkward rebellion across the country, and still a decade from the time they would descend on the Santa Clara Valley and take over the world, had begun sublimating, i.e., networking: quasi-military games like Adventure and Dungeons and Dragons, forming a hacker underground the rest of us would become aware of, at large, only in movies like *War Games*, or, among cognoscenti, in the Society for Creative Anachronism, jousting and raising chalices in the woods. Farmer did a bit of network cracking: "With computers, for some reason," he says, "there's a constant temptation to see what you can get away with." He soon found it a childish waste of time.

Too antisocial even for the misfits, he enlisted in the Marines. Recruiters tried to steer him into computers, but he just wanted to be a grunt: "The ability to blow someone's head off from 150 meters," he later said. "Now that's an interesting skill to have."

"Getting drunk on this," Farmer points gleefully to the second 1978 Barolo we're working on in a pricey Nob Hill ristorante, "is entirely different from the buzz you get on your average bottle of screw-top wine." He summons the waiter for a dessert menu, and his eyes widen when he sees a 1970 Fonseca on the wine list.

Talking to Farmer, particularly about his past, can be frustrating if there's no fine wine on the table. Even drunk, he has an amazing capacity for digression; sober, it's a bit like the hypertext attribute of the World Wide Web—hit a key word and you jettison to some entirely different subject. Questions about his days in the Marines prove especially tough going, for reasons I'm about to experience firsthand.

He lasted through one tour of duty, then went back to school as a reservist, taking a few computer classes, shooting a lot of pool. In 1989, still one course shy of graduating, he took an independent study with Jean Spafford, Purdue's leading computer professor, and wrote COPS (Computer Oracle Password System), a program that tested ("audited") individual machines for security loopholes. Writing the code took three months of all-nighters; Farmer still doesn't understand why he devoted himself so thoroughly. Perhaps it was the rigor the Marines had instilled, perhaps the obscurity of the work: Security was then a virgin field, the provenance of egg-heads employed by corporations and government agencies he was convinced would never have an interest in him. They published papers in small journals that were hard to find, "And even then," he remembers, "you really had to read between the lines. I was offended by the security ethos: People feeling that by knowing something, they had one up on you. The old 'I know that, but if I told you, I'd have to kill you' line. I suppose I also found it very alluring." Perhaps he knew he was on to something: COPS proved a hugely successful tool (one still widely used). Though he gave it away freely, it gained him entrée to the world that had always excluded him. By the fall he was in Pittsburgh, monitoring security nationwide and chasing Internet crackers around the world for CERT (the Computer Emergency Response Team) at Carnegie-Mellon. Later, amid the brouhaha around Satan, he entered negotions with the NSA for a million-dollar contract for himself, a friend, and his former CERT colleague Tsutumo Inomora, the cyberstud who made a name for himself in 1995 by catching Kevin Mitnick. Negotiations broke down when…it really is a long story.

He lasted two years at CERT, getting increasingly fed up with the security mindset. Time and again, he'd alert sysadmins to leaks in their networks, only to see nothing done. "Security through obscurity," he says, "was the modus. Don't mention the problem, no one will know, and you won't have to fix it. CERT was in a great position to become the Ralph Nader of computer security, but it was all so hush-hush: They didn't want to talk about the airbags until after they'd been fixed."

He left in 1991, called up by the Marines for service in the Gulf War. By then, his fervor for long-range genocide had mollified; he petitioned for conscientious-objector status, and spent the eight weeks of the war in Camp LeJeune, North Carolina, carrying weapons with no bullets while his C.O. petition was considered. "One night, I went out to get drunk with two other reservists, and we got to talking about skills we'd learned in Basic Training. 'Oh yeah,' one of them said. 'I'm in a bar, and this guy starts a fight. I pull out my knife, start gutting him, and split. Next day, I read in the paper about this guy who got killed.' Then the other one goes: 'Yeah, I'm in a bar, this guy starts in, I grab him from behind the neck and yank him. Next day, I read in the paper…'"

"He broke his neck?"

"No, crushed his carotid artery. In Basic, hand-to-hand combat training, they bring you to this big sandpit, pair you up into partners. "'OK, we're going to teach you how to kill your partner in three to ten seconds, depends on who they are.'"

Farmer gets up and comes behind me, wrapping his forearm across my neck. "I thought it would feel like blacking out"—he begins to apply pressure—"but it's actually extremely painful."

It is. I look across the restaurant at a tony group of three couples as Farmer tightens up. One of the women is wearing orange haute couture, staring bug-eyed at me; I suddenly find myself wondering if I'm the three- or the ten-second type, if this is the last person I'll ever see. "If I were to just sit down now"—Farmer locks the grip and begins to ease down—"you'd be dead."

Instead, he releases my neck, goes back to his seat, and summons the waiter to order the 1970 Fonseca. The entire restaurant is looking at us. Strange—that I don't feel any resentment, though my neck is ringing with pain; that, with my carotid artery in Farmer's embrace, I didn't feel fear, only curiosity. His voice behind me sounded so logical, his control of the hold so masterful. "I would have no compunction about putting a loaded forty-five to your head and blowing you away," he says, giving me one of those smiles, like Orson Welles in *The Third Man,* looking down from the ferris wheel at all the disposable humanity. "Or that woman over there in the orange dress. What difference would it make if I pulled out a shotgun and ended her life? Mathematically speaking, it makes no difference whatsoever."

My neck is throbbing. I ask Farmer about S&M, and he talks about the relativity of pain, segues into the wise indifference and the capacity for irrationality of Zen masters, then, boom, some word or phrase gets his browser of a brain spinning: "I'm thinking about when my father was terminally ill," he says a few nano-tangents later. "My mother was into holistic healing, and he came home to die. I went to see him, and I told him that I loved him. I always wanted to tell him that again before he died, but somehow that never happened, which upset me. Then I realized, in the long run, what difference would it've made—to him, to my mother, to me? None whatsoever."

"Had you gotten closer to them as you got older?"

"Yes and no. They'd always been so distant, until I started to break away in adolescence, when my mother suddenly took an interest in me: Where are you going? Who are you seeing? I was never able to understand why I'd become so attractive. It was a mystery that nagged. Like when I was younger, first learning about sex. I'd lie in bed and wonder about my parents, over and over: Do they do it?"

"Why did that nag so much?"

"It was a problem I couldn't solve. I've always been that way: When I come across something that doesn't resolve, I stop and won't go further until I've worked it out. Paradoxes are a killer for me."

"Because they're irrational?"

"And because irrationality is as real as reason. It's the line between the two that fascinates me."

"Is that where computers come in?"

"Not at all. Computers aren't necessarily rational. I like computers because they do what I want them to do. If I want to tell a computer that two plus two equals five, it'll spend millions of bytes on that principle. Most of what I want is not rational."

"Is that where S&M comes in?"

"Not at all. S&M is super-rational. My sexuality makes perfect sense to me: Consensual forced sex, with a person who has a fantasy about being overpowered. I spent my life in relationships with partners who weren't enthusiastic about sex with me, until I learned that my fantasies are very real to me."

"Do they involve real pain?"

"Sometimes. It's a fantasy, but when it gets to the actual cuffing and biting and whipping and hitting, it can get pretty physical."

"But you don't enjoy being on the receiving end, do you?"

"Not usually." He reaches across the table to give my arm a friendly squeeze. "But some of my best friends do."

Inside a roped-off area on the second floor of Trocadero, the San Francisco club that becomes "Bondage A Go-Go" on Wednesday nights, a tall, bookish woman in a thong, black leggings, and cheap black flats straddles a wooden sawhorse and closes her eyes. She smiles as her partner, a shlubby guy in a Fu Manchu and pirate outfit, pushes her face down, handcuffs her wrists to the legs of the sawhorse, then whips her thighs and back with an abbreviated cat-o'-nine-tails. On a small stand next to the sawhorse is a fold-out leather case with a set of silver-plated tools—knives, scrapers, pinchers—and several lengths of chain and rubber tubing. When the whipping ends, the tools come out. It starts slowly, punctuated with kisses and whispers; by the time it ends, he's sweating and her body is dotted with red welts. He releases her, and they kiss, rather formally, light up cigarettes, then stand around making small talk. She's a good six inches taller than him.

"Boy, I'd like to top her." Farmer points to a woman in latex, chains, and a rubber apron. "She's truly beautiful." She wields a ten-foot bullwhip on a green-haired man in green leather pants and bustier, hanging a foot off the floor from a swaying leather-and-steel rack attached to the high ceiling. When he's had enough, another man steps into the brace and she gets imperiously back to work. I tell Farmer I don't think she'd be that easy to "top."

"You'd be surprised," he says. "Some of the biggest, toughest dudes and snarliest women turn out to be total bottoms. It takes all kinds."

And they're all here: a 6'7" albino man with large breasts and a page-boy, wearing high heels and hose; a bald woman in men's evening dress, who has apparently had her incisors sharpened to become fangs; a mournful-looking man in a silk-lined red cape and black boxer shorts, who paces among the whippers and torturers zapping himself with a Violent Wand—a miniature cattleprod that shoots a violet-colored charge and flames when it burns. On the first floor, several hundred people in leather, rubber, chains, capes, and baby-doll outfits are dancing to blasting industrial rock. The ambiance is different than one would expect in a club devoted to people working out their dark sides. Everyone seems open and friendly, gathered in a loose, laissez-faire communality, like at an open-mike poetry reading; there's also a strong feeling of unreality, of grown-up make-believe, like at a Star Trek convention. A strange insight: I look at these people and see an entire generation in front of their computers—modular, half at work, half at play, free to reinvent themselves, show themselves without any fear of judgment. I can tell simply by the way I feel. It's clear as day I don't belong here—me with my notebook out and my pen working—but they don't care. It's just what I'm doing.

Farmer does the room like the Prince of Darkness, trailing a heavy musk of clove cigarettes and the thin jangling of his handcuffs, hands in his pockets, charmed by the various types but extremely aloof. Even in this crowd, he's determinedly an outsider, a person who has to disagree. You could clone this guy fifty times, put him in a room with his replications, and he'd still be estranged. Women dressed in black float across the room on stiletto heels on a regular basis to surrender themselves. He kisses them passionately, for about a minute, then very sweetly and pointedly moves on. He has the dominatrix on his mind.

"Are there a lot of computer people here?" I ask.

"Not really. There's one security guy, very well known, who was banned from here for fighting. Now there's a real top. Vicious guy. And there's a woman at SGI that I've been dancing around a relationship with"—he fires up a cigarette as he vaults onto the second-floor ledge and dangles his legs over—"amazingly attractive, brilliant, successful. She can only be someone's slave, someone who'll tell her how to live, dress, think, abuse her. It's so much responsibility, taking control of someone's life. I'm having trouble enough with my own."

"So you don't see much connection between this and the computer world?"

"Not really. The people here are actually looking for something different. Hackers aren't. Like when I was at CERT, I got a call from a military site in Florida. They had an intruder breaking in relentlessly, saying, 'I'm so great, you'll never catch me,' and they couldn't. I told them, 'Just ask the guy for a resume, offer him a job.' He sent it right in, and they busted him. Or when I go to Def-Con at the Sands in Vegas, or these cracker conventions. I get so alienated with these conformists ranting about freedom. I'll give a technical talk to that effect: If you're going to break into me, just please, make it new. I'm tired of these old tricks you guys keep using. Deafening silence. They ask, 'What's your favorite news group?' and there's the same silence when I tell them, Alt.Sex.Bestiality."

"The feeling here reminds me a bit of the Internet."

"That's exactly right. All this talk about the global community and high finance is kind of off the mark. You know how everyone says the Internet is capable of so much, but instead it's just filled with personal garbage? I think they're missing the whole point, which is freedom, the element of fantasy: On the Net you can be anyone you want, say anything, without fear of rejection.

"What I find so strange is that it's all fantasy, both here and there. Here, there's a great feeling, but you can't really call it progress, or even life-affirming. Tomorrow, these people will wake up and be the same mid-management type or janitor that they were before they came in here. And on the Net, I never get anything accomplished. I'm thinking about when me and my partner Wietse were writing the code for Satan: Back and forth on e-mail for months, and we got very little out of it. Finally, I flew to Holland to meet him, and in three days of face-to-face, we polished Satan off."

"What was different?"

"I don't know. What we were doing was purely technical, configuration files and intervals, but somehow it was worthless without the 'human element.' The ability to look each other in the eye and say, 'You're full of shit.'"

The dominatrix, through for the night, walks past us, the long tail of her whip trailing behind her as she heads down the stairs. "Take a hundred people at random," says Farmer, "fifteen of them will be sexually submissive. Every time, I'll pick those fifteen out to desire. Male-female, big-small, black-white, blond-redhead, it doesn't matter: By any rational criteria you'd use, it would seem totally random, but it never fails. I just love that kind of—it's a strange word to use, I know—but I love that kind of verifiability."

"Sounds like science."

"No. I worshipped at the altar of science my entire life. It proved nothing."

The next afternoon, I accompany Farmer down the peninsula to the great altar of Western science known as Silicon Valley. The occasion, a sushi luncheon for the chief researchers at Sun Micro-systems Laboratories, is innocuous and friendly enough, but I quickly begin to feel very old—simply by virtue of having been born five years too early for the spike in the computer-learning curve. I think of a line from an Alain Tanner film: "Prophets make holes in the future that historians look through to see the past." Over urchins, eels, and quail eggs I sit in a room with fifteen people whose work will shape my children's cognitive grammars, and I don't understand a word they're saying, just some quips and atti-tudes from buzzwords I've digested: the implicit condescension of calling hackers "The Mitnick Liberation Society," or a competitor across the Valley "bandwidth challenged"; the begrudging admi-ration of a hacker who broke into a network, changed all passwords to FUCK YOU, set the security level to HIGH, hit ALT, and vanished. The worst insult, it seems, is to call someone "random."

I spend most of the luncheon trying to see how Farmer fits in here, harboring the suspicion his colleagues have a similar diffi-culty. A lot of it, Farmer later tells me, is not his alternativeness, but simple professional conflict. "Their jobs are to improve and in-crease the flow of information. Mine is to make that flow secure. The greater the facility, the greater the security risk."

What they clearly share, however, is an ethos of intelligence, which I begin to realize is the real paradigm shift of this valley: a thorough disinterest in theory, possibility, ultimate truth; a rever-ence for incisiveness, making connections, solving problems. It's a mindset both suited to and dictated by the speed at which the technology is developing: A colleague working on a new chip down the hall, for example, is too busy to join the luncheon, as he's developing a form of three-dimensional calculus to solve a problem created by compressing and decompressing massive amounts of data. At stake, apparently, is the next technological hurdle: Only so much space is currently available to transmit information, ergo the data must be compressed. The work requires a quantum leap from three centuries of math; in five years, perhaps less, the resulting technology will probably be antiquated.

The net result is a breakdown in the normal sequentiality of thought, and with it, an irreverent love of the extreme and a hatred of typical hierarchies. April Fools' Day is a religious event here: They turn people's offices into par-three golf holes, or put steel arrows through the entire building. The pecking order, which seems inchoate at first, is set by skills I would have found hard to predict: On top is neither Farmer, and the publicity he's accrued, or even the resident genius of Research, Whitfield Diffy, who invented public-key encryption two decades ago. Not even the CEO, Scott McNeally, who two weeks previous nearly succeeded in buying Apple. When he stops in for chitchat and sushi-envy, there isn't a look, word, or intimation from anyone in the room that he's any better, worse, or different. But when the name of another colleague hits the floor, the luncheon stops for a half-hour of apocryphal-sounding but apparently true stories of the man's capacity to get things done: how, on a trip to Java to give a conference, he had the harddrive of his laptop fry out on the beach, then found some local maven to scare up a few feet of wire, strips of copper, and a soldering iron. "In two hours," says the teller of this one, "he has it reconfigured, closes it up, hits the button"—he relishes a long pause before the kicker—"and it goes on." Mouths agape through the whole room.

Farmer and I want to smoke—a major no-no in a building that generates vast wealth with supersensitive transistors—and head up to the roof. The vista is both beautiful and ugly: the entire basin brilliantly lit on a warm, still day, but all somehow seeped-over with haze, reflecting between the mountains off the satellite dishes and powerlines connecting the valley's factories and offices.

Farmer hops onto the retaining wall and lets his feet dangle over, then begins telling me who owns what out there: It's like going down the NASDAQ stock pages. I ask if he isn't nervous sitting out on the ledge like that. The question barely registers.

"I suppose I'm a little nervous about you," he finally says. "If you rushed me and pushed me over. But I think I could fight you off."

Something clicks. Of course: Why else would I be so nervous? I have no reason to want to kill Dan Farmer, but the desire is in there somewhere: Anxiety about his futurism and my stone-age intellect? Pure random rage, as the guys downstairs might call it? Or perhaps this random greed I find myself feeling, looking at all these ugly buildings and thinking about the IRA investment I made in technology stocks that's lost me money. "You could break into all these guys, couldn't you?" I ask Farmer.

"Why would I want to?"

"To steal ten million dollars. Or better yet, just find out who's about to take someone over, release something new, buy their stock."

"Difficult, but sure. No problemo."

"How long would it take?"

"I don't know. Somewhere between two hours and two weeks. The two worst things you can do when committing a crime are a) rush into it, and b) not know when to stop. That's how Mitnick got caught. He didn't know when to stop."

"And you wouldn't get caught?"

"No. And if I did, I'd just lie and say I was testing their security, which is what these people hire me for in the first place. How could they doubt me: I'm the long-haired freak who gave Satan away for free."

"Then why not do it?"

"Because I have enough money."

"What about the future?" I ask, still fuming about my languishing retirement plan. "In five years, when the Internet is no longer a fun new game and the big boys have taken over, you might very well be expendable."

"No, I can't be excluded." Farmer gives me the big smile again, this time with a clear sense I haven't understood a word he's said. "The bigger they get, the more they'll need little old me."

Against Witness

William Wenthe

One of us must have a gun,
I said.

Four cars stopped on a desert road,
it's only likely: statistics.

The horse that had been tossed
from the toppled trailer,
writhing, slammed his skull
teeth-first against tarmac.

It hurt so much
to watch: how can I presume
to write it down?

Two shots released him.
Blood. Urine. Shit.

A rope around the neck,
and four men trying to haul
1100 pounds off the road.

It would not give.

A Project for Open City

by Richard Rothman

White House, Staten Island. 1995

Sidewalk and Shrubs, Bay Ridge. 1993

McDonald's with Tiered Landscape, Red Hook. 1992

Precipice, N.J. 1995

Landscape, Savings Bank, N.J. 1996

Driveway, Staten Island. 1992

Front Door with Rhododendron, N.J. 1995

Nursery (Weeping Blue Cypress), Long Island. 1996

Popcorn

Strawberry Saroyan

SHE CLOSES HER EYES AND SEES BLACK AND THEN STRIPES OF COLOR like on television when they do broadcast testing and say this is a test, this is only a test, if this were real…and then the screen disintegrates into a rainbow of microdots swirling around like in a cartoon when someone vanishes into thin air, only this is the opposite of that because the dots make her appear, swirling into an image of her walking down Madison Avenue, and it's her but it isn't really her, she's a movie star circa 1945 and the camera loves her and her style is real instead of just retro, and she's carrying a black cell phone and talking to someone nonstop but the sound is turned down so she can't hear what she's saying, and she worries about it but then she realizes it isn't a cell phone at all, it has a big black cord, shit, she's forgotten to leave her phone at home, but it doesn't matter because the cord keeps stretching as she keeps walking and talking, and the conversation she's having is really important to her movie-star self, but her real self is curious about her apartment so she follows the cord back to her place, and when she arrives it's just like she always thought it might be, it has a chocolate and cream color scheme, it's like walking into a big cup of coffee, it's comfortable, you can sit down, have a drink and there's a rainstorm on the stereo and big abstract paintings everywhere, and she breaks the fourth wall and climbs into a picture of a skyscraper on fire, and once she's inside she wants to get to the top of the building where the flames are so she doesn't even think about it, she just starts flying, she flies standing, it's more like levitation, and when she gets to where she needs to be to save everybody, it isn't actually a building at all, it's a red hot

Rothko suspended in the sky, and she wants out, so she rides a still-wet droplet of paint she finds at the bottom of the canvas down until she hits a lit streetlamp which burns a little but not that bad, and then she lands on the ground, dusts herself off, and starts walking to a dinner party she has to be at on the Upper East Side and on the way she sees a copy of the new *New Yorker* in the window of Hudson News, and she walks in and buys it and her coins clink on the counter, and as they do she hears a faint ringing and she realizes it's the phone but she decides not to get it, and she doesn't but she starts to think she might be awake, and then she starts thinking about her life and what she's doing with it, and the idea of anonymity frightens her like nothing has ever frightened her before, and she is in a slow panic, and she thinks she might as well just commit suicide, the only thing happening is that she'll be 26 and then 27 and then 30, and then her ex-boyfriend appears out of the blue, like changing the channel, looking better than he ever does in real life, looking like a fucking Kennedy, and they're standing on the lawn, and he gives her a copy of his novel and there's an angel on the cover, and she thinks it's weird that he hasn't mentioned her wings but then she thinks he's probably just trying to be polite and she walks upstairs then and flings herself out a window, and she realizes she's falling, but luckily she lands on a bed, and Courtney Love has been sleeping there, but now she's awake and big black cameras with flashbulbs popping but no photographers are pointing at them, and Courtney says let's go into the living room there's a party in there, so they put on matching nightgowns and tiptoe out to surprise everybody but nobody notices, and the Beach Boys are playing but it's all instrumentals, no lyrics, and she starts dancing to the keyboards that sound like they're coming from the future, and then she speeds through a tunnel to a drum solo until she comes out the other side, and then she's at a desk, in an office, and there's a big sign suspended above her that says media slut, and another one that says more, and she starts phoning people she doesn't know and asking them if they still love her and some of them say yes, and the hand she's dialing with has black nails that look like someone stepped on them but they also look chic, and she's smoking a Parliament Light, and she worries about smoking indoors but then she remembers no one cares, it's okay to light up in the office because she's in London, and the thought that she's so far away makes her happy, and she tells the person on the line in L.A., listen we can't talk long because I'm halfway across the world, but then she realizes it doesn't matter because the company's paying and screw the company, and then she walks out to get some lunch somewhere and she sees a white limo, and it looks like Larry Flynt's but someone else rolls down the window and says hi, and she doesn't know who it is at first but then she recognizes Burt Reynolds, looking like he looked in the seventies, and he opens the door and motions for her to come sit on his lap, and she says wait let's take a walk first, I don't really know you, I mean, I know you from the movies but I don't know you as a person and then he convinces her that that's silly she's just scared, and she doesn't want to look scared so she gets in the car, she figures the driver will protect her if nothing else, and then Burt looks into her eyes and tells her to stop thinking, and she does, and by the time they hit the freeway they're making out to the *Mission: Impossible* theme and moving so fast it feels like they're flying, and then she looks up and realizes the car is driving itself, and it's okay as long as they're going in a perfectly straight line but if they come to a turn they're in deep, and Burt thinks the whole thing is funny at first but then he gets pissed because her fear is killing the mood, but she doesn't care, she's going to save herself, so she climbs up front, and the whole time she's praying there are no cops around because she's practically naked and speeding, but then she forgets about it, this is about life and death not traffic tickets and then she gets off on Sunset, and Burt's asleep in the back, and the *Mission: Impossible* disc skips and then dies, but she keeps her eyes on the road and her hands on the wheel, and then the car swerves, and then it swerves again, and she sees the faces of other drivers coming at her head-on but she keeps driving, and then she realizes she's killing people but the brakes aren't working and crashing actually feels kind of cool, but she has to look upset for insurance purposes so she starts faking it, and suddenly she's screaming and crying like a girl in a horror picture, and then she realizes everything is just special effects, the people are crash test dummies and the fire isn't really hot and everyone is still alive, and then Burt opens his movie-star eyes and says don't worry honey, it's all popcorn, and she knows it's a line but she falls for it anyway, what the hell.

I Am a Pizza

Monica Lewinsky

I am a pizza.
I can be a delicious lunch, dinner
or breakfast, if you're weird.
I have a great deal of toppings on me.
I am a round and flat piece of dough
with lots of toppings.
I make your mouth water.
I am very good to eat, but I'm
fattening!
I am a mouth's best friend.
I make you say, "Yum, yum."
I am a pizza.

Courtesy of the 1982 John Thomas Dye School yearbook

**"trusts too readily,
marries too early."**

(Garrison, p.21)

Handsome Pants

Sean McNally

I DON'T HAVE MANY FRIENDS, AND I DON'T HAVE A TELEVISION, SO mostly what I do is, I've got these pants. I call them my handsome pants.

I've got this mirror from the shoe store, you know, that sits on the floor at an angle there? I sit next to it on this footstool I've got, and I look at myself in my handsome pants. It builds my confidence.

When I wear my handsome pants, nothing can stop me, I've got it all going on. I don't in the least bit mind saying that when I'm wearing my handsome pants, it's like as though I'm some kind of President of the United States. One of those fancy ones, I don't know, William Henry Harrison or Kookla Fran and Ollie or somebody. My pants are mighty! My pants are strong! Without them, I'm just kind of a schmo, so I do not, DO NOT go without those pants if I can help it.

They're striking! Very striking! They're not "Hey, how ya doin'?" pants. No, they're "See here! Look here!" pants. They've got stripes in three colors, three colors you've never seen before, vertical, vertical, and three is a magic number, damn you all. I'm uncertain the material, but if it's Tuesday it must be velvet.

They're a little big for me, but I don't wear a belt because a belt makes my bellybelly hang out, and that ruins it, that just ruins it, Pompeii, and so what if I've got to hold them up all the time, Mister One-Handed Pants Boy, holding up his pants. Any clown car sloop john hey abbot silly rabbit knows it's a small price to pay if it makes grown women shake and small men cry.

My pants are powerful, fierce, they don't go with anything. I don't wear other clothes when I've got it all going on, when I'm totally on fire. Underwear would burn beneath these pants, my handsome pants. There's air conditioner microchip mind control laser beam sonic cannon minivan parked outside anti-tree people who'd give anything to get these pants for parties parties I *love* my country and I love my handsome pants. I sit on my footstool and I look in that shoe store angular mirror and I say to myself, sometimes out loud, sometimes I even shout it, I say, "Now these! These are pants!"

Friends and Their Knickers

A Project for Open City

by Ellen Harvey

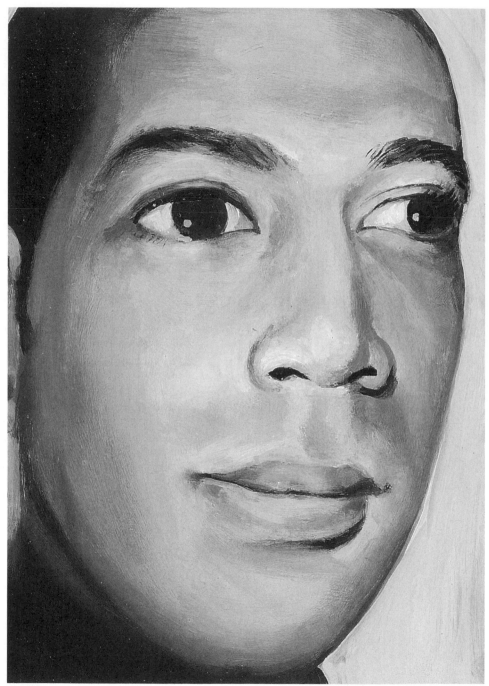

Arfus G.

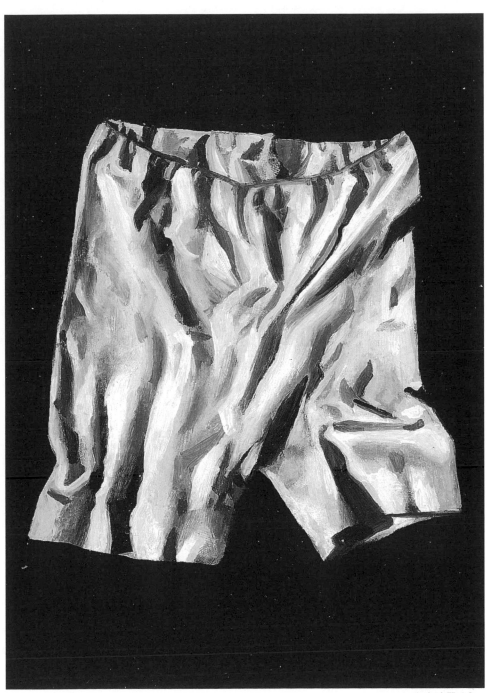

Arfus' Knickers

Ellen A.

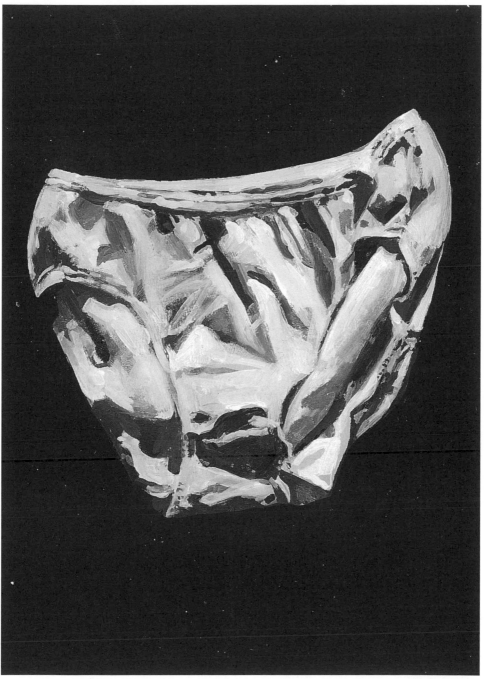

Ellen's Knickers

Jan B.

Jan's Knickers

Brooke W.

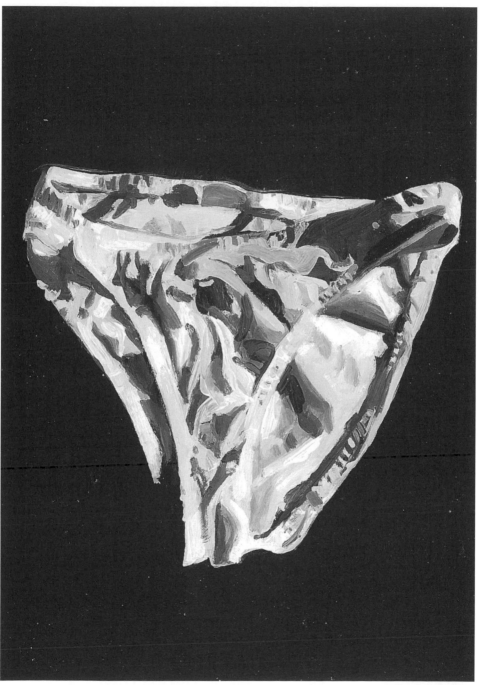

Brooke's Knickers

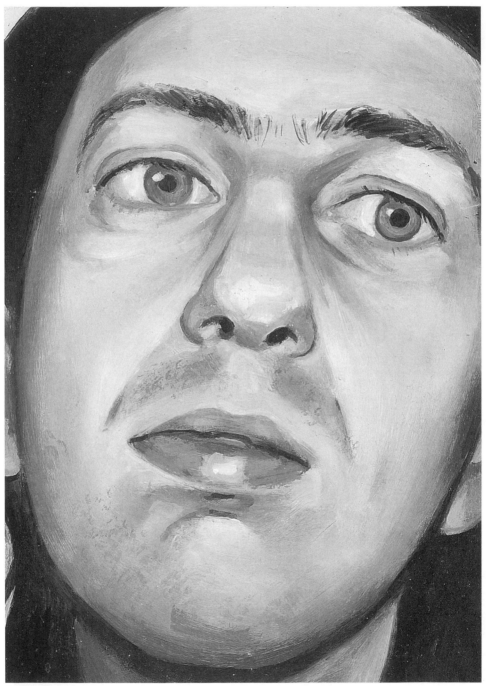

Seamus M.

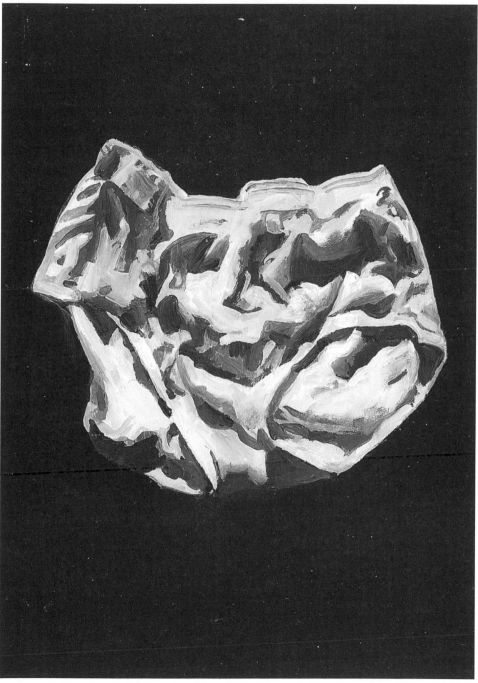

Seamus' Knickers

"I have a great deal of toppings on me."
(Lewinsky, p.129)

Geraldine

James Purdy

SUE AND HER MOTHER BELLE NO LONGER MET IN PERSON, BUT SUE called her mother daily, in fact some times she called her two or three times in a day. The subject was always her worries over her thirteen-year-old son Elmo.

"Now what has he done this time," Belle would sigh or more often yawn.

They had never been close, mother and daughter, and as if to emphasize their lack of rapport through the years, Belle had from his birth taken an almost inordinate delight and interest in her grandson Elmo. She gave him lavish birthday, Christmas and Easter gifts, and of late had begun taking him to the opera. Belle could not tell whether he enjoyed the opera or not but he paid it a strict, almost hypnotic attention and applauded the singers with frenzy. Then they would go off to some midnight cafe and have a dinner of quail or venison.

Belle had heard of course about Geraldine. In fact Geraldine herself came to be very real to the grandmother. The girl, Elmo's girl in Sue's phrase, had the persistent presence of a character in great fiction, though Belle had never met her. At night, under the covers of her bed, Belle would often whisper "Geraldine" and smile.

"They are idiotically in love, and she is at least two years older than Elmo," Sue would report on the telephone. "They are together constantly, constantly. And their kissing! Oh, Belle, Belle." Sue had ceased calling her mother mother for at least ten years. Although the grandmother pretended to like this familiarity it piqued her nonetheless. But then she had never ever been close enough to Sue even to correct her.

"Don't put your foot down," was almost the only advice Belle ever gave her daughter. "Let what will be be. Let him love Geraldine."

Geraldine and Elmo came to an evening Sunday supper one day in December when there was a light, spitting snow outside. Belle was not prepared for Geraldine's extreme good looks and beautiful clothes. She felt she had opened the door on a painting from some little-known Italian hand. Geraldine's eyelashes alone brought a flush to the grandmother's face and lips. The girl's hands free of rings and her arms without bracelets looked like they were made out of some wonderful cream. And then Belle looked round and saw her grandson, not as he had always been on his previous visits but now as a young man with the first show of a beard on his upper lip.

"At last, at last," Belle cried and held both of the young people in succession to her. Tonight she only kissed Geraldine however.

They began going to the opera as a threesome. They attended all of Donizetti's operas that season and after the opera they went to Belle's special cafe and spent hours there laughing as though they were all of the same age.

The crisis came when Sue called Belle at six o'clock in the morning.

"He has had his right ear pierced!"

At first the grandmother thought this referred to an accident of some kind. Only when she was given the explanation that the boy had gone to a professional ear piercer, did she recover from her fright. She broke into laughter at that moment which drove Sue into a fit of weeping, weeping propelled by rage and the revival of the feeling her mother had never loved her.

"No, no, my dear, you must not feel it is a disgrace," Belle advised Sue." It is the fashion for young boys."

"Fashion, my foot," Sue screamed over the wires. "It is Geraldine!" Then Belle as if in spite began even at that early hour to praise the beauty of Geraldine.

A torrent of abuse then followed on the other end of the wire. Sue told of the girl's excesses.

"They do not show, my dear," Belle disagreed. "She is unspotted,

146

unsoiled in every lineament of face and body."

Belle waited with a queer smile on her face while her daughter wept and told of all the shortcomings of Geraldine.

Sue kept a kind of "black book" of Belle's "crimes" against her. She considered in the first place that Belle had usurped her place in Elmo's affections. She had taken Elmo away from her as surely as if she kidnapped him, Sue wrote in her black book. She listed other of Belle's crimes as 1) making Elmo fond of imported sweet-meats, such as chestnuts covered with whipped cream, 2) reading him stories beyond his age group, stories which had questionable morality or contained improper innuendoes, 3) late hours, 4) breakfast in bed after a night of attending the opera, 5) imported hairdressing creams which made Elmo smell more like a fast woman than a young boy, and so on and so on. Then Sue would burst into tears. "Belle never loved me," Sue would whisper to the covers of the black book. Never never so much as one hour did she squander on me the affection she showers on Elmo, or that-bitch Geraldine.

Elmo once called his mother to her face a boo-hooer. That epithet rankled in her heart for a long time. It drove her as if imitating her mother's largesse to go to the most expensive woman's shop in Manhattan and purchase for herself imported hand-sewn handkerchiefs. Into these she wept openly and with uncontrolled wetness. I will boo-hoo both of them, she cried. She even thought of taking legal action against her mother. In fact she called a noted lawyer who dealt in unusual family problems. He discouraged her coldly, even warned her to proceed no further. Then he sent her a bill for one thousand dollars.

"I hate Belle," Sue would often say as she looked out into the garden of her town house. "She will outlive all of us, including Geraldine."

"Your mother says I act like your fairy godmother," Belle said one late afternoon just before she and Elmo were to go to the opera.

Elmo smiled his strange little smile and pressed Geraldine's hand.

"She doesn't mean it as a compliment," Belle told him. "Are you as happy with me, dear boy, as with Sue?" Belle inquired.

147

"Oh a thousand times happier, Belle," Elmo replied. He too had fallen somehow naturally into calling her by her first name.

The old woman beamed. "I would keep you forever," she whispered. "And Geraldine too. Wouldn't we all be a threesome of happy ones," Belle cried. Elmo beamed, and nodded, and Geraldine grinned.

"As happy as larks!" Belle almost shouted. She held Elmo in her arms and kissed him on his cowlick. Then she embraced Geraldine.

"You love Geraldine, don't you?" Belle whispered.

Elmo stiffened a little under her caresses, then in a smothered voice said, "A lot, grandma, a lot."

Whether it was the coming of Geraldine or the desecration of Elmo's and Geraldine's earlobes by the ear-piercing practitioner, Belle was hurtled back in time—what other way could she describe it—to her own youth. She examined her own ear lobes and found that the tiny holes put there so long ago were still ready to bear the presence of her own many earrings. And how many earrings she had! Yes, Sue had criticized her on this score likewise. "You have enough earrings to bestow on a museum," Sue had spoken this judgment on Belle not too long ago. "And you never wear one pair of them."

"But I will, now I will," Belle said aloud today. In her older years she often spent whole afternoons and evenings talking to herself. "But what am I saying. They shall wear them also! Geraldine and Elmo. How I do love them, lord!"

The next evening before the opera the three of them all laughing and giggling and even guffawing began putting on Belle's many earrings.

"Too bad, loves, only one of your ears is pierced," Belle cried, and she showed them herself in full panoply wearing first a priceless set of jade earrings, then the ancient turquoise pair, after that the diamond, and then to the hush-hush of the young couple, her emerald pair.

"O, may I wear the emerald tonight?" Elmo cried.

"Why, Elmo," Geraldine whispered and kissed him wetly on his mouth and chin.

148

"Whyever not, dears, whyever not! And Geraldine must not be left out. By no means. Oh, God in Heaven," Belle cried, "how happy I am. I never would have dreamed two people could have brought me such happiness. Never, never." And she held them to her tightly. "And I don't care what Sue thinks, children," Belle cried.

All at once, as if from a cue somewhere, perhaps from the opera house itself at which they practically lived now, they began dancing all three of them as if in some queer minuet. With their new earrings sparkling, they might indeed have been part of the ballet of some rarely performed opera.

"The only thing that makes sense is gaiety!" Belle cried, a bit out of breath. "If one were never gay, it would not be worth a candle. One must sparkle like our earrings, children! One must sparkle."

Sue's conversion came swiftly and without warning. She had got used to Elmo's always staying the night and often the weekend with his grandmother. In fact Sue began somehow to believe that Elmo now lived with Belle. True, it had always been Belle's wish of course that Elmo stay—really live with her. And since Elmo never went anywhere now without Geraldine, in Sue's troubled mind she assumed that Geraldine like brother and sister both now resided with Sue's mother Belle.

Sue kept touching her ear lobes. The piercing in both her ears which Belle in fact had supervised some twenty years earlier needed attention. The skin in the pierced holes was beginning to close. "I must have them tended to," Sue spoke to herself. Her tall Finnish butler served her course after course tonight all of which she left untasted.

She had stared at Jan the same way at the beginning of every meal when he asked, "Will master Elmo be dining?" Sue would look only at his long blond sideburns and reply, "He is still at his grandmother's."

"I must have my ear lobes pierced again. My earrings don't go in." She spoke aloud within the hearing of Jan.

But that evening came her realization. Unlike Belle, Sue did not hold a box at the opera. But she kept a seat very near the stage which cost more or nearly as much as Belle's royal box. Actually she retained two seats, but Elmo almost never attended the opera with her.

"For where would Geraldine sit, then?" She addressed this statement also to her Finnish servant.

He could hardly wait until he reached the safety of the kitchen to burst out laughing to the cook. Sue heard his laughter but construed it as coming from his asthmatic attacks. "He wheezes like an animal," she once remarked to Elmo. "If he weren't so tall and personable I would ditch him."

She arrived late at the opera but tipped the usher to allow her to go in against regulations when the opera was in progress.

No sooner had she disturbed 40 or 50 people gaining her seat than her eyes swept away from the stage to Belle in her box. "Ah, ah," she cried again disturbing the opera lovers. She had never seen anything so resplendent! There they were, Belle, Geraldine and Elmo, but with what a difference. Each wore earrings, each wore some kind of shining necklace attached to the beads of which was a resplendent kind of brooch. Sue wondered why every eye in the opera house was not watching Belle and her retinue.

Sue wept unashamedly. She never heard a note of the opera. But her weeping refreshed her more than a dive in a cool spring. The vision of her loved ones for she now knew she too loved Geraldine almost as much as her own flesh and blood, that vision dissolved then and forever her jealousy and rancor. She suddenly accepted Belle and with her acceptance of her mother she accepted her jurisdiction and sequestration of her son and her son's sweetheart Geraldine.

"Let them love one another," she cried and falling back against the rich upholstery of her seat she went to sleep.

She was awakened by an usher shaking her. The opera had long been over, every seat but hers emptied. Looking up at Belle's box she saw it too was deserted, extinct of resplendence.

She was helped out to the street by the usher who summoned her a cab. She gave him an ostentatiously grand tip, and sped away in the cab.

"Tomorrow, I will have my ear lobes re-pierced," she spoke loud enough for the cab driver to hear. He nodded gloomily.

I wanted to please her, yes, Sue reflected after it was all over, I saw I wanted only one thing, to be Belle's little girl .

The world-famous jeweler was not too surprised as he had been Sue's jeweler for twenty years when he saw Sue enter his private consulting room in the jeweler's shop—a room reserved only for the phenomenally wealthy.

"My dear, you look tired." He helped her to a green French settee. "Shan't I get you something?"

Sue could only nod. He brought her out a dark liquid in a glass so thin it resembled mere paper but sparkled like diamonds. One would have thought he knew she was coming, had prepared for her visit days in advance.

"I saw the earrings in the window," Sue only moistened her lips with the brandy.

"I had hoped you'd come by and look at them," Mr. Henton-Coburn confided.

"I want to please Belle," she brought out. "My husband spoiled me so I wouldn't bother him. Every time he felt I was going to ask something of him I got a gift. They were mostly jewels as you know. He purchased however very few earrings. I will need all the earrings on display."

"But two are spoken for."

She put down her glass, and touched her lower lip.

"But if you insist of course."

"I said I wanted them. I mean I have to have them. I have to please Belle...."

"But, listen, dear friend," and she took a noisy swallow of the brandy. "I think" (she placed a finger on an ear lobe) "they need piercing again. When I had my trouble, my sorrow with Belle, I all but quit wearing jewels."

"May I?" he inquired and bent over her left ear. Then her right ear.

"What is needed, dear lady, is," and he produced a kind of stiff thread. "I will pull this through with your say-so where the old piercing was and you'll be perfect for the displays in the window. Oh, my dear, why haven't you been by?" He bent down and kissed her.

Her decision to attend the opera then one snowy bitter night with the mercury near zero ushered in what resembled, as she later noted in her book of records, what resembled different ceremonies, a first communion, a wedding, perhaps even a funeral. But it was none of these. It was more—she blushed as she wrote it down—like going to paradise.

She had spent hours on her toilet. She had tried on at least fourteen pairs of earrings.

That night at the opera looking down with his opera glasses Elmo caught sight of a woman who looked somehow familiar yet the more he gazed at her the less sure he was it was anyone he knew. Yes! Looking again he saw that it was someone who resembled Sue, yet this Sue was wearing the most elegant and ornate earrings he had ever seen anybody wearing.

"Is that Sue?" he inquired of Geraldine.

Geraldine took the opera glasses and looked only a moment, then merely shrugged her shoulders. Elmo stared at Geraldine coldly and Geraldine returned the stare with a frigid contemptuous expression in her eyes and on her lips.

Belle now took the opera glasses and looked down. But at that moment the house lights dimmed and soon the overture to the third act began.

Geraldine and Elmo had quarreled. And Belle had become distant, as if her real center of affection now was Geraldine and not Elmo.

It was snowing harder when the three of them left the opera house. Belle looked at Elmo inquiringly as he summoned for them a cab.

"I will not be coming with you, Grandma," Elmo spoke with devastating aplomb. Helping Belle into the cab, he almost pushed Geraldine in after her. Belle was too surprised to protest, or even say anything but, "Goodnight then."

"I am going home," Elmo spoke aloud; his mouth opened wide and received the thick goosefeathery flakes of snow. "It was Sue, I know that, with her ears pierced."

"Yes, so it was you."

Elmo had entered his mother's room on the top floor as he said this. He was so covered with snow, his eyebrows and the hair sticking out from his ski cap white as avalanches, even a few hairs in his nostrils white.

Sue had just in fact put on an even more resplendent pair of earrings as if she was waiting for him to see her so arrayed. When as a matter of fact she thought he would stay on indefinitely with Geraldine and Belle.

"Mother, good evening," he said. He sat down on the divan near her.

She was still too astounded to speak and his calling her mother further stopped the speech in her throat.

"Take off your wet clothes and put them in the bathroom to dry."

"I can't get over it," he said obeying her and going into the bathroom, a room as large as many New York parlors.

He looked at himself in the mirror. To his astonishment or was it astonishment really, anyhow he saw that his own earring had disappeared from his ear lobe. He touched where it had been pierced.

Coming out of the bathroom he gazed at Sue. She looked almost as young as Geraldine and yes, admit it, Elmo, he thought to himself, admit it, more lovely.

"Well, Mother," he said again.

"What has brought this about?" Sue wondered. "Shall I wake up Jan and have him prepare us something?" Elmo shook his head.

"Geraldine is through with me," he began. He sniffled a bit whether from the snow or his grief was not clear. "Finished, finito."

"Ah, well, that is what being young brings," Sue said.

"And Belle prefers her to me."

"Oh, Belle," Sue said. Then minding her speech she merely added. "Well, she's old."

"And fickle," he added. "The opera is her lifeblood."

"Certainly the costumes and the sets are. She's deaf as a nest of adders."

"Belle is deaf?"

"And nearly blind."

"How many earrings do you have?" he wondered.

"I'm afraid enough for everybody in the opera.

"Do you mind if I stay with you now, Mother?"

"Nothing you could suggest would make me more happy."

Two huge tears descended from her eyes.

Elmo sat back astonished, some wet snow drops falling from his thick black hair. His eyelashes too long for a boy's as Geraldine had pointed out, sparkled with wetness.

"And you won't send me away somewhere."

Sue shook her head and mumbled, "Never."

"May I kiss you then?" he wondered. He came over to where she sat limp and disheveled for all her jewels.

"Mother, I believe…"

"Don't say any more."

But he finished his sentence. "I feel I'm home."

Ideas of Order at Key West

A Project for Open City

by Eric Lindbloom

Ghost Palms, 1998

Ft. Zachary Taylor, 1998

Shuttered, 1998

Vallum Interruptus, 1998

Fallen Frond, 1998

Southernmost Point, 1998

Nice Cool Beds

Hunter Kennedy

FRANCE WOKE UP IN THE COFFIN-SIZED COOLER. HE VAGUELY remembered pouring the water down Honeycut's steps. It was early still. He shambled down to his house in wet clothes and found his father asleep on one of the rollaway beds in their yard. Crisco's neck was pimpled with mosquito bites. France crept past him down the dock into the house. He changed clothes, but he was still wearing a hangover. On his way through the kitchen, he bumped into the refrigerator. Their house looked small as a fist in the morning glare. He stuck his mouth to the tap and drank.

France was in no hurry to tell his father that the Thunderbird was back. He wanted to let Crisco find it parked out front this afternoon when he was well away from the house. His father would assume Uncle Terry had returned it, not that France had pried it back out of Uncle Terry's fingers. He hoped his father might also decide to start looking for his own place. The benefit of Crisco leaving definitely outweighed losing the car. France was trying to smoothly work out his father's departure, but it was delicate business. Crisco would be offended, even betrayed, if he knew that France was behind the delivery of the car.

The breeze was blowing in from the Atlantic and a pleasant salt tang hung in the air. France walked through the weeds into Honeycut's side yard and found the Thunderbird lodged between boxwoods in clear sight of the road. He re-parked it in the shed, hoping Crisco hadn't already seen it. The tail end of the cottonmouth was still in the footwell of the backseat, curled in a hook. He worried another moccasin was still coiled under the seat, so he quickly grabbed the snake tail and flung it at the dog. With a sharp bark, the muddy springer snatched up the limb and trotted off, tail wagging. France rubbed his eyes and followed. He had so much to do.

Wrestler Jenney's Icehouse was a five-minute drive in the crab truck. Most of the shrimp from McClellanville bound for Atlanta first passed through this door. France remembered hearing, perhaps from Crisco, that Wrestler had gotten his start driving a shrimp truck. For as long as France could remember, trucks had been parked here waiting for ice. The older black men were already sitting outside of the icehouse in folding chairs when France pulled into the shell lot. Wrestler had a son as old as France who now handled all the loading, and the pair seemed particularly representative this bleary morning of how he and Crisco should have been behaving. Wrestler was grinning when he stepped out the cab. France winced.

"Your house ain't burn down yet?" razzed Wrestler as he shook hands with France. Wrestler's son Previous flashed a mouthful of gold caps when he chuckled.

"We're still working on it."

"Your place won't burn. It's too fulla salt water, puts itself out. But if it does, I'll let you sleep here with the shrimp. Don't think they don't have sweet dreams! These shrimp have nice cool beds."

"Maybe I ought to move in with y'all," replied France. That had them rolling. Previous could hardly pour the ice. The older gentlemen slapped their bony knees and shook.

France spent the rest of the morning hauling in the traps. The blue crabs stubbonly hung on when he dumped the last cage into the tank, so he gave it a couple extra slams. He liked how crabs never gave in to the cold fact that their number was up until they hit the kitchen. They had no idea the sweet dreams ahead of them, but for that matter, he admitted, neither did he. When he pulled up the boat, he heard hammering coming from the house. He found Honeycut nailing in the last of the new plywood panels, sawdust in his hair.

"I had nothing to do," he shrugged. "Your dad just walked to work."

"Tell you what, eagle eyes. I'm going to park the Thunderbird out front, and if Crisco comes home before I get back from delivery, tell him Uncle Terry dropped it off."

"I don't know a thing about it."

France delivered crabs to a fleet of restaurants between George-town and McClellanville, but his first stop was always the oyster bar. Rich met him at the back door in a white suit, and he was already reaching for his money clip.

"France, give me the biggest blue crabs you have."

France reached into the icy well with the tongs and filled a bucket with granddaddies, their claws crossed like pharaohs. The owner poked a stick at them and tipped France a fifty. He always tipped high.

"Gotta keep them off of somebody else's plate, France. Thanks."

"Anytime."

"By the way, I was telling your story at lunch and one of the wait-resses insisted I have you come in. She says you won't remember her. Her name's Ce Ce."

"You're kidding me. I haven't seen her in years."

"You're in for a nice surprise, man."

Ce Ce Long was the girl at the marina boat shop who had given Honeycut a black eye for talking bad about a shrimp boat her brother happened to work on. He and France had both tossed change in the Mason jar for her tuition fund like the rest of them, and when that pretty wild child left for college, most gave a sigh of relief. France had no idea she was back. He edged into the bar uneasily, shakily, suddenly remembering how much of a crush he'd had on her.

She shouted, "Hey, Francis!" and hugged him before he could even say her name. He decided right there to let her do all the talking from here on out.

"You and I have got to sit down and have a couple cervezas, man. I've heard all these things about you that can't possibly be true! It's so good to see you. You're finally filling out."

So there were women in this world. He agreed, through an exchange of hand signals and nods, to meet her that night when she was off shift. He rushed to the other restaurants, his head buzzing with static, her face on the screen. He wanted to look into that face all night.

France Dieter studied the quarter-sized hole burned into the floor of his crab shack. His father Crisco had done that with a dropped cigarette. Ever since Crisco had moved back in, things like this had been happening. The tabletops were tracked with filter length burns. His father had given up on crabbing for good and now worked at a fireworks stand out on the highway. The house was loaded with fireworks, and France could feel a fire coming, as though the gunpowder had gotten into their clothes. The marsh water glittered through the hole in the kitchen floor, and a fleck of light moved back and forth like a minnow on the ceiling.

When Crisco got back from work, France didn't offer him a cigarette. His wiry father noted this and produced a half a pack of Kools that he had pinched off of his teenaged supervisor. He tossed another bag of Black Cats in the corner and sauntered to a chair. France ignored his satisfied grin and studied a tidal chart, impatient for a rising tide. The momentum was against him. Crisco shook a cig into his lips and scratched a matchbox with a scarred middle finger. The Sure Strikes chattered like a bucket of agitated crabs. Crisco lit the crumpled Kool, sighed, and before France could point a finger at the ashtray between them, flicked the match over his shoulder. Crisco was aiming for the open doorway out on to the marsh, but the lit match hit the shaving mirror and disappeared. Twin bottle rockets shrieked past their heads, lighting a bag of bottle rockets lying on the TV. The room filled with roaring lights as Crisco's fireworks collection ignited. France danced an unpracticed shag step as he tiptoed through spinning lotus flowers, jumping jacks, and paper tanks.

"Christ in a motherfucking Chevy! Where's the damn hose!" cursed Crisco as he ran out the door.

"This is the last goddam time I do this."

France rushed down the dock with the writing desk and dropped it in the weeds. He pulled the picture frames off the wall, threw the lawn chairs in a stack in the grass, and ran back for his bed. He and Crisco's beds had hospital wheels. He flicked the brakes and quickly wedged her out the door into the smoke filled den, where the air was as white as an old woman's hair and thick enough to choke on. A last set of jumping jacks exploded under his feet, and the lights buzzed between his bare legs and bounced under the springs. A curtain caught fire, and Crisco wheeled around to douse it. France rammed the bed out the front door and down the warped dock.

France hopped on the back of the bedframe and steered the rolling bed into the street. He was headed to Honeycut's house, sure the flames behind him were licking at the sky. Just a few mailboxes up the street, the house was banded by a dark screened porch, and from the road it was hard to tell if Honeycut was on it. France shouted as he skidded into the patchy yard.

"Honeycut, we got another fire."

Honeycut appeared with a pair of binoculars around his neck. His face, neck, and arms, like France's, were brick tan from time on the water. He had a red handlebar mustache and was regularly pegged for an Allman brother.

"Looks like your daddy's got it back under control," said Honeycut as he focused the binoculars. "Maybe you ought to get him some of those nicotine patches."

France laughed bitterly and shot a glance back at their shack.

"He'd find a way to light them."

Honeycut handed his friend the binoculars, and France surveyed the scene from the bedframe. Crisco was sweeping sparklers into the water. Smoke plumed out of an open window. In a way, France Dieter didn't give a damn what happened to the house. It was half porch anyway. But from this distance, he realized that was a smaller part than the side of him that viewed the shack as the only thing Crisco had ever given him. He had earned that gift.

France scratched his chest and softly ticked off the checklist of things undone while one of Honeycut's dogs bit at his ankle. The daylight was already beginning to dwindle down to the pink of a dog's belly. Honeycut shouted at the dog in his booming voice, and it slunk away into a mound of untrimmed boxwoods. They walked together down the road to the shell lot. The dog circled them warily and ran ahead down the row of blackwater oaks that framed the road. Their limbs tangled above the unpaved street in a slanting net of shadows. France knew this row of oaks once led somewhere, but he would hardly say that now.

The damage to the crab shack was pretty minor, considering. They had to rip a couple of plywood panels out of the corner, and the top of the TV had melted from the heat, but it still worked. Crisco stressed that. He flipped through the channels while France and Honeycut ripped out the last panel. Mosquitoes were pouring through the hole in the floor into the room. This fire had unlocked something awful. France knew he would not be able to sleep.

"Dad, at least open some windows."

"I was just about to do that. You always were psychic."

"Jesus. Cut off the TV."

They ate greasy barbeque sandwiches at Honeycut's house. Crisco walked into town to get drunk with the firemen. France asked if Honeycut still had a typewriter. His ex-wife Traci had in fact just returned it. Heavy as an anchor, it was kept in a back room next to a coffee can full of broken, thin-bladed boning knives. France shut the door behind him and pecked away at it for a solid hour. When he re-appeared on the porch, Honeycut offered him a beer from a coffin-sized ice chest that used to hold billfish. France sucked half the beer down noisily and rubbed the can on his forehead.

"I wouldn't mind lying down in that," he said.

"Did you write a letter to somebody?" asked Honeycut.

"Dad pawned the phone. I needed to focus."

"You can use mine. Who you calling?"

"Uncle Terry."

France picked up his thick Woolworth's address book and started leafing through it for Terry's number. Notes and phone numbers were scattered like birdshot through the book. It was a loose but traceable organization that spread beyond the maze of marsh channels into the connecting world. It seemed to France that the only place his life held any order was between those covers. He found the number on a bare page in the back labeled FAMILY. Honeycut handed him the phone and France took it into the hall. While France was out of the room, Honeycut stared at the book, tempted to pick it up. The letter's edge glinted like a knife blade between the singed pages. He wondered if France meant business, but before he could see for himself, his friend loped back into the room.

"Let's go tonight. Let's get my damn car."

"Guess it was busy."

They took Honeycut's station wagon. The bearings whimpered as they pulled out the yard. France parceled out the directions a turn at a time. They drove away from the coast into the thick smell of pines. Outside Yemassee, they turned up a dirt drive that went for a mile. The pine stands were so thick that they lost sight of the moon. Moths showered their car.

"What does your uncle do out here?"

"He's got a turpentine farm."

"Christ, Crisco's brother is Mr. Clean."

"Not quite as clean as he'd like people to think."

They slowed at the mouth of the tunnel of pines. A large white house with scrolled columns hunched in the clearing. Crisco's Thunderbird was parked in the weeds next to a log pile. Honeycut parked beside it and left the motor running. Cicadas and crickets rumbled through the woods in a frenzy as France walked up to the front door. Uncle Terry was waiting for him.

"I was fixing to let Little Terry take that car to school with him," he said. "You know he's off at Baptist Southern, and he says he needs it for dates. I guess you came at the nick of time."

They shook hands. His uncle smelled of pine pitch and chicken livers.

"I apologize for showing up so late. Dad got a job with a seafood wholesaler and needs it in a hurry." The lie tasted coppery in his mouth, but he didn't mind. He liked lying to his uncle.

"How about I give you the keys to the Monte Carlo? Runs better than anything else I own. Like I said, Little Terry likes that Thunderbird. Been driving it, what, a year now. What do you say, Francis?"

"It's not mine to give," said France flatly. "Give me the keys."

The keys caught the light when Terry held them up. He dangled them in front of France. France simply held out his palm.

"Crisco doesn't need that car."

"Oh, he does. He's got his license back and he's itching to go."

"Fine, take the damn thing on short notice. Just get it out the yard."

He dropped the keys and walked back inside. Little Terry had been watching the proceedings from a nearby window. When France saw him, Terry flipped him the bird.

They stopped in an oyster bar in McClellanville. France and

168

Honeycut were only a few miles from their street, but they were drunk, and distances were stretching away from them. The owner, an effeminate, Napoleonic character named Rich, had been feeding them beers all night. He was delighted by France's story: his house had caught fire, and he had driven a car an hour with a moccasin curled in the back seat. The bar owner still had a taste for risks. He'd just retired from dealing coke, and he missed it.

"When did you find the snake, France?" he asked, leaning forward on his fingertips.

"In your parking lot, Rich. I shut the door on him."

Rich sprang back, his fingers hooked in front of him like bear claws. His asthma was acting up, and he was flushed.

"Another round for these gentlemen!" he announced and staggered away to find his inhaler, wheezing.

France sped home to take a shower. When he arrived at the shell lot, he found Crisco scrubbing the hood of the silver Thunderbird with an old undershirt. Crisco, from the looks of him, was drifting in a reverie of all the cars he had ever driven, a long trail which zigzagged up and down the Sea Islands, strewn with broken glass, loose change, and blind dates. It had been oft repeated, just like the legend of his fateful encounter with France's mother on that Charleston city bus. France slammed the door to get his attention.

"It looks like a damn yard sale, dad. How about we move some furniture."

"Don't you see this car, France? Your uncle's slathered it in sap."

"I want this stuff in the house tonight. I'm going to take a shower."

The sun had sunk into the hair of the pines when France re-emerged combed and clean. He had managed to pry most of the pluff mud out from under his nails and had broken out a pair of white bucks. Crisco cocked his head in mock disbelief.

"You kidnap a businessman and trade clothes?" he snorted.

"Got a date with Ce Ce Long."

"Oh yeah, the dancer. Tell her your old man was stationed in Seville in '61. I can still dance flamenco."

"You can tell her that yourself," responded France.

"Well now, I just might. When should I be expecting her?"

169

"Do that on your own time. You know, I haven't had any guests out here in a long while. We need to work something out."

"I guess you're right. Shit." Crisco lit a cigarette and tossed the match in the creek, deftly avoiding his son's even stare.

"We might be swinging by tonight. What are you going to be doing?"

"Don't worry, I'm not going to be in your hair. I'll probably go prowling."

France's stare softened a bit.

"How about leave me a note," said France in a low voice.

"If I can find something to write on, I will," said Crisco with a touch of defiance.

"Don't take it the wrong way, Dad," said France as he walked away. "I just need a little bit more room to move."

"I'll throw in a little map, too," replied Crisco, "so you can navigate."

Crisco went back to buffing details with a rag, his shoulders taut. A brassy little radio tooted on a nearby cinder block. France had hoped to leave him on a good note, not this blues lick. He walked to his truck in the glowing dusk, hounded by the riffs.

He picked up Ce Ce at the oyster bar and drove her back to her apartment complex. She sorted through blouses while he watched cable in the next room. Then they drove to an old fish house back on the Santee River that most tourists hadn't managed to penetrate. Over flounder and beer, they caught up on lost time. France explained as briefly as possible the incidents surrounding Crisco's midlife collapse. The fact that his old man had quit crabbing to sell fireworks floored her. He didn't mention the fact that Crisco's supervisor was a teenager.

"Is he living with you now?" she asked, fork suspended in mid-air.

"Yeah, he's been back for about a year. He'd given me the house, but it wasn't long after he quit crabbing that he had to move back in. Didn't want anything more to do with it, but won't quite move aside."

"How long do you think he's going to be there?" ventured Ce Ce.

"We're working that out." France chewed thoughtfully, then added, "As we speak."

A stray group of golfers wandered in as they finished their

plates, and the one in pink slacks put some quarters in the juke-box. After a song, Ce Ce asked France if he wanted to dance. On any other night, he would've said no, but he followed her to the clear spot in front of the dented jukebox. They shagged to a few songs, holding on by one hand as they scraped their feet to the beach music. The guy in pink broke on him just as he was getting the hang of it, so he watched her from the bar with the other golfers. She floated above the sawdust in the icy jukebox light.

"Let's get some cervezas somewhere else," she said. On their way out the fish house, Ce Ce ran into one of the waitresses from the oyster bar. Her hair was the color of hornets, and her hands were excited and shaky.

"One of the Allman Brothers came by right after you left, Ce Ce. I mean, it was crazy. We even talked."

When they were out on the highway, France explained.

"Remember how you gave my friend Honeycut a black eye?"

"Course I do. He had it coming."

"Well, since he grew out a mustache, people have been getting him confused with somebody talented. You've got to see him."

They found Honeycut at the bar next to Rich, taking hits off of his inhaler. The bar was dark as a closet, but France could see that Rich was still in his white suit. He was telling a story about doing lines with an albino hit man in Savannah as he sipped a white Russian. Previous Jenney played guitar in the corner, accompanied by two cousins from the icehouse on backbeat and rhythm. They sat in cane chairs under a lone shaded bulb, their music crawling out the speakers between everyone's legs. The nameless song in-spired France to order Ce Ce and the rest of them bourbon shots. Ce Ce and France made a clink of their glasses, and she touched his arm. Honeycut handed the inhaler back to Rich, who grinned like a silver fox. France wiped his mouth and ordered another round. Previous throttled the guitar neck like it was about to strike. France thought of his father and hoped there weren't any more snakes in the car.

When Previous quit playing, they drove back to Honeycut's. Ce Ce wanted a tour of the block. When they met Honeycut in the yard, he pointed up at the kitchen window and shook his head. A light was on in the kitchen. Honeycut said, " That's my ex-wife's calling card. She's come for something." The springer padded up through the fireflies to sniff Ce Ce's calves. She played with the springer on the porch while Honeycut uneasily hunted through his ring of keys. France got them all beers out of the billfish cooler.

"All right, let's start this tour," growled Honeycut. "I hope there's no surprises."

In the living room, he pointed out the high school trophies. Some of the arms had been broken off, and when Ce Ce asked if the damage was from a hurricane, Honeycut chuckled and scratched his chin.

"That would be my dear ex-wife. She threw that state champs one there all the way into the guest room, but you can't hardly tell after I superglued it."

Honeycut quickly led Ce Ce and France to the guestroom and cut on the light. The typewriter was still there, and Honeycut did a quick count of the boning knives. They walked into the kitchen, Honeycut in the lead. France hoped she hadn't trashed the kitchen again.

There was a pound cake on the counter.

"Jesus." Honeycut gave a deep sigh.

They had a slice of cake on the porch and listened to the cicadas revving in the blackwater oaks. Not a car passed. France was fidgety with the thoughts of his father's conversation. He began to think he had been a little hard on Crisco. Ce Ce noticed his anxiousness and got him another beer. Honeycut had walked into the yard, and it was just the two of them on the billfish cooler. He told her about the house filling with sparks, running down the road on the back of the bed, having to tear out the floor, knowing she would hang onto the words.

"Wrestler Jenney claims our house would never burn, but I should go down and check on the place."

"Let me go with you, Francis. I want to see it."

"Okay, walk down with me."

A second later, the screen door slammed behind Honeycut.

"All the lights are out at your place. I bet he'll be gone for a long while," he announced.

"Nah, he's just gone prowling," said France.

"He's probably dreaming of cheerleaders in North Charleston

as we speak."

The fireflies hovered like a drift net electrified as they walked the dim road to the crab shack. France was quiet and a little wound-up. He hoped the furniture hadn't been stolen. Ce Ce peered out for what he was searching for, letting her arm brush against his. The night was hot and still, its weak light grainy and distorted by the wings of a thousand insects churning out of the marsh. Whispering, they crossed the empty shell lot, drinking in the dark house's every detail. The planks creaked, the hermit crabs scattering. He let go of her hand at the front door, only half-aware that it had even been held. His mind was on his father's note. She followed him into the dark.

The room jumped into focus with a click of a light switch. The furniture was heaped haphazardly in the big room. Chairs lay on tables, photos hung at angles. There wasn't a note. Ce Ce started to re-arrange the furniture while France looked around the kitchen for a scrap of paper. He didn't see one. He checked the counters of the tables in the living room, on the back and front porch, even the shaving mirror. It occurred to him that Crisco might not have found anything to write on. When he checked his room, he found a crumpled piece of paper on the sheets of his rolling bed.

"Wrestler Jenney took me on. Bring the bed to Jenney Ice when you get a chance. Stretch out and double down. Signed in a hurry, Crisco."

He looked around the room for his address book with the singed pages. The fact his father ripped a page out of a book to write a note pissed him off. It was another attack on perfection, an assault on his own sensibilities, but so Crisco Dieter that he had to smile. France folded the note into his wallet and quietly walked into his father's room. There was nothing left in the closet but coat hangers and a couple empty matchboxes. The dresser had been stripped. The trunk of the Thunderbird was probably filled with fireworks. He sat down on the edge of the bed and took a deep breath. This was what he'd wanted.

For a few moments he forgot about Ce Ce until the sound of a scraping chair shook him from his thoughts. He jumped to his feet and walked back to the living room. She had completely re-arranged the room, and the furniture was in a different constellation. He didn't see her anywhere, and for a cold second, he was sure she'd left. He walked past the couch, then wheeled around. She was lying on her side, ashing in her shoe.

They made out in the blue light of the television for several commercial cycles. She slept beside him on the rollaway in her clothes. In the morning, when she woke, he had already been out in the boat. The other bed was lying legs up in the back of the truck. He gave her a cup of coffee and asked if she wanted to take a ride. She did. He took her to Wrestler's. After a night's sleep, the tension was gone in France. He seemed light as driftwood, and his salty hair stuck out in tufts. When Previous walked out from the landing to meet them, France called out to him.

"What's all this smoke out here. Mr. Crisco didn't already burn this place down?"

"Pop's just trying to teach the man some tricks on the grill."

France and Previous rolled the bed into the cooler, through heavy doors, into Previous' little practice space. Crisco's clothes were everywhere. When they walked back out the garage doors, Wrestler, Crisco and Ce Ce were standing out by the truck. Crisco was busy proving he could still flamenco.

The Slap of Love

Michael Cunningham

THIS IS THE STORY OF ANGEL SEGARRA, A PUERTO RICAN KID FROM the South Bronx who became Angie Xtravaganza, doyenne of the drag world made briefly famous by Jennie Livingston's acclaimed 1990 documentary, *Paris Is Burning*.

Angel, neé Angie, died in New York City on April 6, 1993, at the age of 27.

She died of complications from AIDS, but she also had chronic liver trouble, probably brought on by the hormones she'd been taking since the age of 15 to soften her skin and give her breasts and hips. She'd lived for over ten years as her own creation, a ferocious maternal force who turned tricks in hotel rooms over a bar called the Cock Ring and who made chicken soup for the gaggle of friends she called her kids after they came home from a long night on the town.

The hard facts about Angel neé Angie are scarce. She believed in her ability to eradicate the past, to be renowned simply and purely for what she had made of herself. She had reason to believe it was possible. As she lay dying, RuPAul was becoming the first drag queen to have a record in Billboard's Top Ten. Lypsinka had appeared in a Gap ad and was about to open at the Cherry Lane Theater, a legitimate off-off-Broadway house that seats six hundred.

Angie refused to talk about her childhood, to anyone. She'd never been a scrawny boy named Angel Segarra, one of 13 children, most of whom had different fathers. She wasn't the son of an abusive Puerto Rican woman in the South Bronx. She hadn't had a rotten, violent childhood haunted by Catholicism. She was and had always been triumphant, dazzling, the fiercest thing in high heels.

I started my search for the true story of Angie with Dorian Corey, 56, a legend in drag circles and one of the stars of *Paris Is Burning*. I arranged to see her for the first time at Sally's II, the drag bar where she emceed a show a every Thursday night.

Sally's II, just off Times Square, is a hustler bar for men who prefer their men in dresses. It's a gaudy, threadbare joint where drag queens, not generally of a recent vintage and some downright geriatric, aggressively peddle themselves to skeevy-looking guys who look as if they have unhappy wives and a few fucked-up kids and a little patch of dying lawn somewhere in the suburbs. It's a destination, the last stop on the train, and you'd have to be a deeply dedicated romantic to find any appreciable element of glamour there.

Corey's show took place in a largish room behind the bar proper, a leftover from some other incarnation, its walls covered with faded murals of Edwardian men and women cavorting heterosexually. The room was furnished with scarred garden furniture—wobbly white plastic tables and molded plastic chairs.

Corey's show started 45 minutes late, at almost one A.M. Although the bar up front was crowded, only four or five of us sat scattered among the lawn chairs, and everyone but me seemed more interested in his drink or his cigarette or some vaguely upsetting dialogue going on in his own head. Sally himself, a raging canary-yellow blond missing his front teeth, introduced Dorian, and she appeared from behind the Masonite partition that served as a dressing room.

Though you'd have to have been legally blind to think of Dorian as a beauty, she was undeniably spectacular. Six feet tall, she had on another foot and a half of silver hair. She wore more makeup than some women apply cumulatively over their entire lives. Her low-cut black bugle-beaded gown showed a few stray curly hairs nestled in her silicone décolletage.

She lip-synched a rendition of "Georgia," walking the edges of the dance floor with the bulky, unswerving grace of a steamship. She was a focused if not an inspired performer, and she made glacial, unrelenting eye contact. She dared you to dislike her act.

After her opening number she picked up the microphone and shouted toward the bar, "It's showtime back here, you girls don't know what you're missing." But the girls were doing business. Dorian gamely introduced a couple of other queens, whose style was more in the classic drag mode: torchily animated, sexualized, exaggerated. Then Dorian performed her stately closing number, "Stormy Weather," and that was that.

I followed her back behind the Masonsite partition and introduced myself. Pop music was cranked up right after Dorian's show ended, and her rickety dressing room stood next to the deejay's booth. The music was so loud I could feel it humming in the Masonite when I touched the doorjam.

"Ah, the writer," she shouted. "Hello, baby."

She grandly extended a red-nailed hand. She was already tucking into a rum and Coke.

"Thanks for agreeing to do this," I shouted back.

"You want to talk about Angie?" she said.

"What?"

"You want to talk about Angie?"

"Yes. You knew her, didn't you?"

"What was that?"

"You knew Angie. Didn't you?"

"Sure I did."

The music was rattling the makeup bottles on the plywood counter. I suggested we go someplace else.

"It's awfully late," Dorian hollered. "Why don't you come up to my place next Thursday? You can interview me while I get dressed for the show."

I told her I'd be happy to do that. When she asked me to repeat myself I simply nodded, and she wrote down an address on West 140th Street, in Harlem.

Angie's drag career began at the age of 14, in 1980, when she was still more or less Angel Segarra. Though drag hasn't exactly become a middle-American value, it's come a long way since 1980, when Madonna was just another easy girl from Detroit and most gay men wore mustaches and polo shirts. Back in 1980 it was mainly just Angel and a ragged band of kids, all black or Hispanic, hanging out in the Village and going to the drag balls, where Dorian Corey was one of the reigning stars. Dorian was capable of turning up at a ball as Marie Antoinette, complete with farthingale run up on her portable sewing machine, life-sized guillotine, and a wig just slightly smaller than the fountain in front of the Plaza. She was capable of wearing three gowns, one right on top of the other, with a 30-by-40-foot feather cape, so that once she'd shed the gowns and gotten down to her sequined body stocking, two attendants could raise the cape up on poles and produce a feathered tent that sheltered half the audience.

"I just took everybody in under my dress," Corey said.

On the drag circuit, she was fabulousness incarnate. She was one of Angel's early role models.

Angel always snuck out of his mother's house with his other clothes in a shopping bag. Riding the subway down from the South Bronx he'd slip a skirt up over his jeans, dab on eyeliner every time the train stopped moving. Angel's favorite place was the piers at the end of Christopher Street. The piers are dilapidated, covered with graffiti and old furls of chain link fence. Through holes in the planks you can see the brown water of the Hudson. Across the river, among the trees and high-rises of New Jersey, the neon Maxwell House coffee cup tips over to spill its two bright-red drops of coffee over and over and over again.

Angel spent most of his evenings there. He was one of the regulars, a wiry, sharp-witted kid—no one's idea of good-looking—with acres of attitude and a fashion sense that could cut glass. He was just another apprentice drag queen, a Dorian Corey in the making, dancing the nights away. He picked up whatever clothing allowance he could get from johns who'd go for style and spirit, who didn't insist on beauty.

Angel was a tough kid, without a speck of sentimentality. But he did have depths. And he had a kind of radar.

As David Gonzalez, one of Angie's adopted children, says, "She was so for real, she could pull a fake in a minute. Someone that's false, she could pull him out in a minute. She would never embarrass anyone, but after they left, she'd be, like, 'She's not for real.' She just knew. And you knew that she knew. And if she thought you were a fake she wouldn't have nothing to do with you."

But if Angel liked you—if you didn't set off his minutely-honed bullshit detectors—he was yours. Forever. Whether you treated him well or not.

If he liked you, he was your mother.

One of the people he liked was a handsome 20 year old named Hector Crespo. Hector was another of the guys who kept turning up at the piers and hanging around the balls. The youngest of 12 children, he had been on his own since he was 13.

"I started hanging out around Christopher Street when I was nine," Hector says. "There were always fights in my family, always drugs, my brothers were dealing drugs, but never where my mother could see it. When she found out there was drugs in the house, she threw my brothers out. She was that strict. But she still told me she'd rather I be a drug dealer than be gay.

"My first experience with a guy, I was seven. When my mother found out I was gay, she started treating me like shit. She was, like, 'You want to be a woman, start cleaning up.' I was treated like a slave. So I ran away. I ate out of garbage cans, slept in abandoned buildings."

By 1980, when he was 20, Hector had tried twice to kill himself. After the second unsuccessful attempt, he decided maybe he was "here for a reason, like, God has something for me." He quit performing in hellish drag clubs like the Collage and the Magic Touch in Queens, got a minimum-wage job at a quasi-health food store called Yogurt Delite. He started the long work of trying to survive his childhood.

On weekends he headed for the piers, to be with the people who felt most like family; to listen to their radios, trade insults, cruise the boys. He got to know Angel, casually at first, just talking. Then they got to be better friends.

Hector says, "Sometimes when I was tired, I'd sit down on a bench with Angel and she'd say, 'Why don't you sleep?' And she'd make me put my head in her lap. We'd stay there like that for an hour or more, talking. It was never boring. When I said something stupid, she slapped me."

They sat on the benches night after night: the exhausted twenty year old who'd been living on his own since he was 13 and the stern little feminine boy, not yet 15, who cradled him.

Later that summer, on a hot afternoon, Hector went to the far end of one of the piers to inhale the watery air, to get himself a shot of relative quiet. After a while, Angel sat down beside him and said,

"What's the matter? Where's your mother?"

Hector answered, "I don't know, I think she's at work."

Angel wore mascara and a red bugle-beaded skirt. "You don't know where your mother is?" he said. "Your mother's right next to you."

"No, my mother's at work," Hector said.

"No. I'm your mother," Angel told him.

Pushing fifteen, Angel was on her way to becoming Angie, mother of the House of Xtravaganza.

A year later, Hector was clipping happily along Christopher Street when he got nailed. It was a summer Saturday night, and Hector was working an outfit: short shorts, high tops, a tight black T-shirt. He could smell the river up ahead; he could feel the night's sour promise blowing through.

He'd just crossed Hudson Street when a hand landed on his ass. A mouth hovered beside his ear and told him where it wanted to put its tongue.

It was some Jersey geek, a big one; a truck-driver type, in tight jeans and poly-blend tank top. Christopher Street was full of guys like this. They'd swoop into the Village, pick off a Hispanic or black kid, jump back into their cars and vanish back through the Holland Tunnel.

The guy had a hand like a shovel. He'd scooped up Hector's ass and was pushing him along, narrating the twenty minutes that lay ahead. He had the money in his other hand.

He'd guessed wrong about Hector, though. Hector was just out for the evening, prettied up, looking for adventure. He told the guy to get lost. He made it clear that he wasn't just playing hard to get.

The guy pulled his hand back and started hollering. "Fucking faggot, get away from me. You little slimeball."

Hector hurried on, left the geek shouting insults. This sort of thing happened all the time, but it still threw a shadow on the evening. There was always a feeling of threat. If a guy like that got really crazy, if he flagged down a cop and told him Hector'd been soliciting, who was the cop more likely to believe? A family man from Hoboken, or a half-black, half-Puerto Rican kid in shorts the size of a pot holder?

Down at the Christopher Street piers, Hector ran into Angel, who by then had changed his name to Angie. Angie was done up for Saturday night like the Christmas tree at Rockefeller Center, in a glittery dress and what would become her signature accessories: drop earrings and seven-inch stiletto heels. As a matter of principal, Angie refused any shoe with a heel shorter than five inches.

"Hey, Ma," Hector said. All her friends called her Ma, even though, at the time, she was not yet sixteen.

"Hi, honey," she said to Hector. "How was your day?"

Angie didn't speak in elaborate, biting wit like most of the rest of the queens. She was straightforward. She had no fear of ordinary conversations—her own hard flash was enough.

"Fine," Hector told her. But Angie knew something was up. She could smell unhappiness the way a chef can smell a sauce starting to curdle.

"What is it?" she asked.

"Nothing," Hector said.

"Don't lie to your mother. Talk."

He talked. Angie never had to ask anybody twice. He told her about the creep and assured her it was no big deal.

"Come on," Angie said, taking his hand.

"Where we going?" Hector asked.

"We're gonna find that motherfucker."

Hector would have been happy enough to let it pass. He didn't want trouble; he just wanted to dance with his adopted family and dish the dirt. As Angie dragged him back toward Christopher Street he tried complimenting her on her hair and outfit, hoping to distract her; hoping that in the name of her own splendor she'd decide against risking breaking a nail or dislodging her French twist. But once she got pissed off, Angie was as soft and reasonable as a hydraulic staple gun.

She pulled Hector down Christopher Street until they spotted the guy, lounging around in front of the convenience store on the corner of Bleecker, chugging a beer and cruising for prey. He was even bigger than Hector remembered. Angie strode up to him in her seven-inch heels, her dress glittering like a school of minnows.

" 'Scuse me," she said. "Did you call my boy a faggot?"

The man swallowed beer, looked at her as if she was something he'd just picked from between his teeth.

"What's it to you?" he said.

"'What's it to me? He's my son, that's what."

"What do you want me to do?" the man said.

"Apologize. Now."

The guy didn't bother to stifle a belch. After a moment, Angie told him, "Do what I say. Don't let the dress fool you."

"Fuck off," the man answered.

Then Angie, at five foot eight, under a hundred and fifty pounds, was on him. She could punch with the skill and precision of a professional bantamweight. The guy doubled over, spewing spittle and hot, meaty wind. His beer bottle cracked on the sidewalk.

Angie saw that the message had been received. She said to Hector, "Okay, now. Run."

She and Hector took off. Angie was fearless but she wasn't stupid. And she could run almost as well as she could fight. She kept up with Hector, even in those heels.

"I warned you," she called over her shoulder. "Don't let the dress fool you."

On a Wednesday night in 1993, I got home and found Dorian Corey's voice on my answering machine.

"Mr. Cunningham," she said imperiously. "I naturally assumed you would call before you came. I'm not feeling well. Please call at your earliest opportunity."

I called her the following morning—drag queen morning, which to most other people is three in the afternoon.

"Mm-hm?"

"Dorian? It's Michael Cunningham."

"Oh, Mr. Cunningham."

"I'm sorry you're not feeling well."

"I'm afraid I won't be up to an interview."

"All right. Maybe next Thursday."

"Yes. Maybe next Thursday."

"I'll call first."

"Please do."

"I hope you're feeling better."

"Thanks, baby."

Everybody needs a mother. Some of us get one who loves us enough, who does more or less the right thing. Others of us decide to become the mother we didn't have.

The House of Xtravaganza, like the House of Corey and the other houses, consists of a mother and a father and a big raucous band of "children": drag queens, butch queens (gay men who dress like men), transsexuals, a few real girls and one or two straight guys. The smattering of girls and straight guys notwithstanding, the houses are, essentially, cabals of young gay black and Hispanic men obsessed with being fashionable and fabulous.

The houses started in the late sixties. They grew out of the underground drag balls that had been going on in and around New York City since the thirties. Those balls were merely drag fashion shows staged by white men two or three times a year in gay bars, with prizes given for the most outrageous costumes. Black queens sometimes showed up but they were expected to whiten their faces and they rarely won a prize.

Says Pepper LaBeija, 45, another enduring star of the drag ball circuit, "It was our goal then to look like white women. They used to tell me, 'You have negroid features,' and I'd say, 'That's all right, I have white eyes.' That's how it was back then."

In the sixties a handful of black queens finally got fed up and started holding balls of their own in Harlem, where they quickly pushed the institution to heights undreamed of by the little gangs of white men parading around in frocks in basement taverns. In a burst of liberated zeal they rented big places like the Elks Lodge on 139th Street, and they turned up in dresses Madame Pompadour herself might have thought twice about.

Word spread around Harlem that a retinue of drag queens was putting together outfits bigger and grander than Rose Parade floats, and the balls began to attract spectators, first by the dozens and then by the hundreds, gay and straight alike. People brought liquor with them, sandwiches, buckets of chicken. As the audiences grew, the queens gave them more and more for their money. Cleopatra on her barge, all in gold lamé, with a half dozen attendants waving white, glittering palm fronds. Faux fashion models in feathered coats lined with mylar, so that when the coat was thrown open and a two-thousand-watt incandescent lamp suddenly lit, the people in the first few rows were blinded for minutes afterward.

It was Vegas comes to Harlem. It was the queens' most baroque fantasies of glamour and stardom, all run on Singer sewing machines in tiny apartments.

Gradually, as the Harlem balls became an underground sensation, the drag queens started splitting into factions.

In 1977 an imperious, elegant queen named Crystal LaBeija announced that a ball she'd helped put together was being given by the House of LaBeija, as in House of Chanel or House of Dior. It was a P.R. gimmick, something to add a little more panache and, not incidentally, to increase the luster of Crystal LaBeija.

The concept caught on, and suddenly every ball was being given by a house. Some queens named their house after themselves, like Avis Pendavis' House of Pendavis or Dorian Corey's House of Corey. Others took the names of established designers like Chanel or St. Laurent.

And once those queens had declared themselves the official royalty of drag society, it was only a matter of time before they began to attract followers. By the early eighties younger, less experienced drag queens were declaring themselves members of this house or that house, and competing in balls under the house name. Some went to court and had their last names legally changed, to Pendavis or Corey or Chanel or St. Laurent.

The ball circuit turned, by slow degrees, into a team effort, as much like organized sports as it was like show business. Houses came to be ruled by their biggest stars, who were known as mothers and who exhorted their members—their children—to accumulate as many prizes as possible for the greater glory of the house.

It was three weeks before Dorian Corey was feeling well enough to see me. She lived on the top floor of a snug, four-story, red-brick row house across the street from the City College of New York campus. It was a nice block, well maintained, not at all the residential equivalent of Sally's II. I was relieved, for Dorian's sake.

I rang the bell, and Dorian's voice, which registered somewhere between the sound of an oboe and a pair of pinking shears, wafted down from the top floor.

"Stand out in the street, honey, and I'll throw you the keys."

I stepped out into the street, and a plastic change purse landed at my feet. I took the keys from the purse, let myself in to a clean, crumbling lobby that had been elegant eighty or ninety years earlier. A matronly brown fireplace and mocha-colored wainscoting gave way, at shoulder level, to yellow-green paint and sputtering fluorescent light. I walked up the four flights. I'd brought a dozen pale pink roses.

Dorian met me at the door. If you'd have had to be legally blind to consider her beautiful in full makeup, you'd have had to be legally dead to consider her so without it, in a knee length T-shirt, with her hair wrapped up in an old nylon scarf.

But her dowager manner held. She formally invited me in, accepted the roses without comment, as if my bringing them had been assumed. Grocery boys brought groceries; reporters brought roses. She led me into the living room, introduced me to her lover Leo, and disappeared, saying she'd be back soon.

Leo was a sparse, wiry man in his thirties who bore more than a passing resemblance to Charles Manson. He wore jeans and a baggy shirt. He was watching a Knicks game on television. Dorian's and Leo's living room was a grotto dedicated to the goddess of junk. In the spaces between the television, the sofa, several chairs, and a double bed, only a narrow footpath remained negotiable among displays of old crockery, embroidered pillows, assorted lamps, artificial flowers, and gilded trophies won by Dorian at various balls. It was a yard-sale version of Aladdin's cave.

Leo watched the game with an acolyte's rapture. When a commercial for Kool-Aid came on, he told me brightly that he'd bought some just the other day. He jumped up, trotted out of the room, and came back with a large can of something called Pink Swimmingo. It depicted a flamingo in sunglasses, snorkel, and jams.

"See?" he said. "Pink Swimmingo. Not fla-mingo. Swimmingo."

"Uh-huh," I said. "Well."

Soon after, Dorian returned and said to me, "Are you ready to be rescued?" I told her I was, and she beckoned me into her sewing room.

Dorian's sewing room was a treasure cave of a different order, more like the real thing. Or, rather, it was a more faithful fake version of the real thing. Strands of faux pearls and rhinestones looped out of shoe boxes. Leopard prints and gold-threaded gauzes and sequined chiffons were piled everywhere, and in the middle rose a dressmaker's dummy wearing a half-finished contraption of rhinestones and flesh-colored ultra suede, a hybrid of early Bob Mackie and late Road Warrior.

We spent slightly more than three minutes on the subject of Angie. Dorian said Angie had been fabulous, a great mother and a promising star. Dorian, unlike some other drag legends, was generous toward her sisters. But still, it quickly became apparent that you didn't go to one major star for detailed information about another. So we talked about Dorian.

She was one of the "terrible five," the five reigning house mothers of the ball world. Angie had been another, along with Pepper LaBeija, Avis Pendavis, and Paris Dupree, whose annual ball "Paris is Burning" gave Livingston the title for her film.

"I used to have a lot of children, but time passes on. Those children who used to come by and talk, they're now the mothers of their own houses. I'm an over-the-hill legend, you know? Leo in there is really the only child I've got left. He was my lover for the first four or five years, then he was my friend the next twenty minutes, and now he's my son."

From the other room, I could hear Leo happily cheering on the Knicks.

A house can be composed of a hundred or more children, or as few as one. There are now at least thirty official houses in New York City, and their membership requirements vary. In some houses, you have to win a prize at a ball to be considered for membership. In others, all you have to do is ask the house mother, who will probably say yes.

Members of the House of Xtravaganza are a little vague about their own prerequisites. "We know right away if you're an Xtravaganza or not," says Danny Xtravaganza, thirty-four, who replaced Angie as house mother after she died. Adds Mina Xtravaganza, eighteen, a straight female member and aspiring model, "The only real requirement is that you be fab."

About being fab: You should dress wonderfully, in a style that's both unique to you and right on the razor's edge of fashion. You should have a mystique, a snap, a sparkle. You should click, immediately, with the other members of the house.

And you must—you absolutely must—look like you can put out some serious competition at the balls. The Xtravaganzas carry on Angie's two overriding fixations: fashion and perfect performance. The balls are the family business, and the Xtravaganzas are as serious about apparel and presentation as the De Beers family is about diamonds.

Over the past decade, the balls have moved steadily downtown from Harlem. Today most of them are held in Village clubs or in midtown community centers. They've evolved from costume parties into enormous multi-categoried competitions that can go on as long as twelve hours. Contestants compete in a numbing array of categories, from best body (with butch and femme subcategories) to realness (most convincingly female, most convincingly butch, etcetera), military (most convincingly lethal), high fashion foot and eye wear, and etcetera.

There can be dozens of categories in a single evening: best wig, best butch queen walking in drag for the first time, best dressed for a night at the Clinton White House. There are even special categories for very short drag queens (midget model's effect), and those who weigh over 180 pounds.

The balls have become intricate, searingly competitive affairs, though they no longer attract the body of spectators who used to show up in Harlem. Now almost everyone who comes is there to compete, and has paid 20 bucks at the door. Some of the trophies are 12 feet tall. The grand-prize winner can take home a thousand dollars or more.

Dorian had amassed over 50 grand prizes. I asked her whether she had a favorite outfit and she paused with a look of mingled pride and regret, like a mother being asked if she doesn't really have a favorite among her children.

"Well, this was quite a while ago," she said. "I made a rhinestone gown, then I had a headpiece with rhinestones all over it. I had a backpiece maybe about nine feet, covered with white feathers. Then I made two smaller ones about 7 feet high, diamonds, and covered them with feathers and had little hand grips. So now I'm getting to be about 20 feet wide and 15 feet high.

"I'd rented a fog machine. They turned it on and the whole stage filled with fog, and I folded those two sidepieces in front of me and I came out and as I got to center stage I opened them and it made the fog part. And everybody gasped. I wanted to run down and see me too. It was the only time I'd ever walked a ball that I had no doubt I'd won."

The competition gets ferocious. As in organized sports, the tension that accumulates around all that desire, preparation, and rivalry sometimes explodes. People really want those trophies—accumulating trophies is the only way to become a star like Dorian. They really want the grand-prize money too. As Roger Milan, father of the House of Milan, puts it, "Some people have medical bills, some people have rent to pay, and they go to the balls telling themselves, 'I must win.'"

Pepper LaBeija says of a 1991 ball held at the Marc Ballroom on Union Square West, "One of the children pulled out a knife and cut one of the judges because he didn't give her a ten. Everybody went crazy, there was a stampede. I ran out in the street in my gown, with my hair in a bun, and it was pouring. The gown got heavy, it got waterlogged, but you had to run. If you didn't, you'd get trampled.

"I'm in the street, one shoe on, one shoe off, and I ran into the subway station."

Even if you don't get hurt at one of these affairs, you can end up sitting in a subway train with your hair askew and your gown soaked, minus one of your pumps. It's a hard world, like every other world.

Angie Xtravaganza was an upstart, the youngest of the legendary mothers; from the moment she started walking balls, though, at the age of sixteen, she was a star. She came up with a new angle. If luminaries like Dorian and Pepper LaBeija relied on flash and audacity, Angie pushed her fashion sense. She didn't put together big outlandish costumes, as drag queens had been doing since the day the first man slipped into the first gown. She shocked the ball world by doing something no one had done before.

She won trophies by dressing in bold but impeccable taste.

Her favorite category was model's effect, in which the prize

188

goes to the contestant who most convincingly impersonates a fashion model. She was famous for her legs, and for her perfect imitation of a runway model's walk. Danny Xtravaganza recalls one of her triumphs:

"She wore an eggshell-colored linen suit, a mini-skirt and a blazer, with brown trimming and brown buttons," he says. "She had a brown organza blouse underneath the jacket, and a white duster and a brown shawl."

The ensemble, like most of her outfits, had been made for her by one of her friends. When Angie walked for the judges—a panel composed of members of various other houses—she got ten points from each of them, the maximum score. As is often the case, several other contestants racked up perfect scores too.

Whenever that happens, the battle begins in earnest.

The game goes into overtime. Sudden death. All the finalists come out at once, and each of them does whatever she can to convince the judges that they have no reasonable choice but to give her the trophy because she is, simply, inarguably, the most potent vision of shimmering perfection.

Danny says, "Angie went to the middle of the runway and started spinning. And the shawl she was carrying got bigger and bigger and bigger. The first time she walked, it just looked like a regular little shawl, but it turned out to be, like, fifty feet long. She started swinging it, and all the other queens got tangled up in it."

She lassoed those bitches like a cowgirl bringing down heifers. And she did it without tottering for a moment in her six-inch heels. Don't bother to ask if she won that night.

The ball world is changing, as worlds inevitably do. For one thing, the drag queens are thinning out and the butch queens are multiplying. Dorian said, "When you have gay liberation, certain things get lost in the shuffle. It's coming out of the closet, so there's no mystique."

It's true that old-fashioned standards of feminine behavior seem to be disappearing, One example of the newer breed of drag queen is Consuela Cosmetics, a friendly, forthright figure roughly the size of a Chevy Impala. She's the mother of the new House of L'Amour, and she resembles Dorian and Angie to roughly the same extent Fergie resembles Queen Elizabeth II. She likes leather and bondage. She's six-foot-three, with silicone breasts the exact size and shape of honeydew melons. She wants to be the first transgender crossover artist. When asked about her duties as house mother, she says, "I'm the decision-maker. I'm the president of the house."

None of that maternal business. Forget chicken soup.

"The House of L'Amour is an association," she says, "and we all get together and compete in the balls against other associations, like the Xtravaganzas and the Milans."

Years ago, Consuela ran a prostitution ring in Los Angeles until the heat got turned up so high she slipped out of town. "I was a supervisor," she says. "Directing traffic."

Were most of her stable transvestites?

"Uh-uh. Pussy makes money. I had real girls and I had a sex change. Pussy wins overall."

She drifted around Europe for a few years, and has now landed in New York. She designs clothes. She sings.

"When somebody says, 'Have you ever known one of the girls who really made it?' I want my name to pop up. Because if you asked that question now, nobody could give you an answer. They can say a whole lot that were fabulous, but we're talking about circulating in the right places, being seen constantly in the media. And no, I can't think of one. And I know queens from hell to breakfast."

What about RuPaul?

"I'm not talking about no RuPaul, with no wig on, and be a bald–headed man in the daytime. I'm talking about transgender."

Angie started taking hormone shots when she was 15. A doctor who called himself Jimmy Treetop, now in prison, used to work the clubs where the drag queens hung out, places with names like Crisco's and Peter Rabbit's. Jimmy Treetop would sell you a syringe full of female hormones and vitamin B-12 for $15, or a kit of six shots for $60. Angie, like most of the other queens, bolstered the hormones with estrogen and progesterone, which she took in the form of birth control pills.

It's important to go on hormones early if you want to look convincingly female. Wait too long, grow too old, and your face and body take on their masculine angles. Begin the hormones after age twenty and the best you're likely to do is end up looking like a man with tits.

Angie, at fifteen, was transformed. It's a twist on the Cinderella story. As Hector says, "Thank God for hormones, because she was very much a beasty little boy. It's like, you are ooh-la, honey. But she started wearing her dresses and stuff like that, taking her hormones, and hormones do soften you up."

Angie never became a classic beauty, but with the help of hormones and a sense of style she acquired a sleek, glowering presence. She had the limitless self-assurance that can pass for beauty simply because its owner betrays not a kilowatt of doubt. Think of Cher showing up half-naked at the Academy Awards. Think of Anjelica Huston anywhere, under any circumstances.

Angie believed in bearing and grooming above all else. She used to say, "If you're going to look like a lady but act like a faggot, why bother?"

All the legendary mothers have had breasts and hips created with hormones or silicone, but have kept their male genitalia. They live in a gray area between genders.

Dorian said, "I had silicone. I found this doctor in Yonkers who was doing silicone, this was back in sixty-seven or sixty-eight. He did a silicone injection instead of a silicone implant, which is what I should have gotten. But that called for one chunk of money, and with the injections, for thirty-five dollars you could get a double shot, and then when you had some more money you could go back and get some more. 'Til you were happy."

Dorian didn't start drag until her early twenties but was made a mother at the age of eight. Her own mother, who'd divorced Dorian's father when Dorian was very young, remarried and was only too happy to let her precocious son take over the maternal particulars. When Dorian was in the third grade her mother had a baby and simply handed it over.

"She set the baby down and showed me how to diaper it," Dorian said. "Now, remember, I was eight. She showed me where the formula was in the refrigerator, and how to heat it, and how to test it on my wrist. And kindly informed me she'd be home at midnight."

Angie Xtravaganza was a loving mother, if a little peevish about

191

expressing her softer emotions and remorseless in her enforcement of the rules. As the children clamored around her—as fifty-plus grown men called her Ma and vied for her attention—she sometimes lifted her face to the ceiling and hollered, "I should have had abortions." But she never lashed out at the kids with any real seriousness, and the kids knew never to let her get too angry. They teased her and, if teasing didn't work, they simply obeyed.

Says Frank Xtravaganza, thirty-one, another of Angie's children, "Angie would always scream your name across a room. Her voice was so shrill, it'd cut right through you, and we'd go, 'Ma, those hormones didn't help your voice any.' She'd be sitting on the sofa, and she'd laugh and go, 'Shut up, you damn butch queen, and get me a cup of coffee before I get up from here and beat your ass.'"

She was joking. But still, somebody always got her the coffee.

Angie's AIDS was diagnosed in 1991, when she was 25. Within a year she was going regularly to St. Claire's Hospital to have the fluid drained from her lungs, and she felt so depleted she moved out of her own apartment to live with Frank on East 94th Street. Angie and Frank used to break the night together back when she was still Angel Segarra. During the six months she lived with him she grew emaciated. She was covered with Karposi's sarcoma lesions. But she still wore her trademark dangle earrings. She put on makeup every day, and got a wig when her hair started falling out from chemotherapy. Throughout her illness she remained stern, bossy, affectionate, and reluctant about showing too much emotion.

Frank recalls, "Angie hated to be patronized, even when she was sick. She'd say to people, 'You're just being nice to me because I'm dying.' I saw her whimper maybe twice, and it lasted, like, three minutes. I'd cry and go through changes and she'd say, 'I wish you wouldn't do this to me.'"

A mother, to Angie's mind, was regal. She didn't get weepy with her children, or they with her. She loved them. She ruled them. She took care of them. End of story.

"The last time she went out," Frank says, "it was St. Valentine's Day. I'd had a date, but he stood me up, and I was bummed about it. Angie, she was really sick by then, but she said, 'Miss Thing, we're going out.' She put on makeup and her wig. She wore jeans and a top that showed her belly button, which was about the only place by then that didn't have k.s. lesions. She teased up her wig, sprayed it, and we went to the Sound Factory Bar."

A drag mother will not only buck you up when you're feeling rejected. Unlike most other mothers, a drag mother will spray her wig and take you out herself.

Around that time, Hector Xtravaganza was going home from work when he heard a couple of queens from a rival house talking about Angie. He was waiting at the light on Sixth Avenue. He'd been thinking about Angie—those days he thought of little else and suddenly he heard her name.

"Oh, Angie, she's a bitch. I wish she'd hurry up and die."

It was a couple of kids with dyed orange flattops, being hateful as only kids can be; waving their cigarettes like Gloria Swanson, throwing some shade on a Tuesday night.

Hector flipped. He grabbed one of the kids by his clear plastic jacket, threw him down and kicked him, hard enough to send a bright thread of blood unfurling onto the pavement. The other one screamed and started to run, but Hector caught his shoulder, spun him around and pummeled him in the chest and face until the kid crumpled and knelt quietly in the street, bleeding onto the Versace silk shirt he'd been planning to wear to the upcoming ball.

Hector started seeing a psychologist, who ordered him to stay away from Angie during her last days. Watching Angie die was too much for him, the shrink maintained. After all Hector's years of scrapping around, this was the thing he might not survive.

Some of the other children visited her faithfully. Some were too frightened by the prospect of seeing her sick. Up to the end she advised her kids about what to wear to balls, and she was willing to do it by telephone with the ones who couldn't bring themselves to see her in the flesh. She claimed she didn't mind.

"She was a mother right up to the end," Frank says, and he's probably right. Like a lot of mothers, she was comforted by some of her children and abandoned by others. Like a lot of mothers, she seemed to have carved an identity out of a devotion so unstinting it borders on the inhuman.

During her last weeks Angie liked to say, à la Piaf, "I have no regrets." She usually added, "No drag queen has carried herself the way I have. I'm not a beauty but I've got class."

She died alone, at night, in the hospital.

I had an appointment for a second interview with Dorian the week following our first conversation, but she had to cancel again, pleading ill health. We agreed to get together when she was feeling up to it. That was the last time I spoke to her. I left messages on her answering machine, which she never returned. I knew, from some of the children, that she was in and out of St. Luke's Hospital.

She faded quickly over the summer. Her mind frayed and started to untangle. She grew sulky and silent; she wanted few visitors. Having been generous and expansive, a vast presence, all her life, in death she curled herself up like a fist. To the children's chagrin she offered no deathbed wisdom. She grew angry and incoherent. She didn't part the fog grandly, in a gown of white feathers. She died at home, with Leo the sweet-tempered man-child and his brother, whom she'd taken in after his own parents kicked him out.

In *Paris Is Burning*, she delivers the film's coda as she applies makeup to a face that looks as much like the pocked, ravaged surface of a planet as it does like flesh.

"I always had hopes of being a big star," she says. "But as you get older, you aim a little lower. Everybody wants to make an impression, some mark upon the world. Then you think, you've made a mark on the world if you just get through it, and a few people remember your name. Then you've left a mark. You don't have to bend the whole world. I think it's better just to enjoy it. Pay your dues, and just enjoy it. If you shoot an arrow and it goes real high, hooray for you."

After Angie died her ashes were sent back to the South Bronx, with the name Angel Segarra on the plaque. It seems that our pasts have a way of reeling us back in, no matter what we do or how far we travel. Still, our created selves, however short their shelf lives, can leave legacies behind. They are small legacies, but they're legacies nonetheless, and ones that we could never have offered if we'd just stayed home.

Hector, for instance, has survived Angie's death. He's got a job with a fur company in Soho, an apartment of his own in Brooklyn. He keeps what he calls a "death album," filled with memorabilia of everyone he loves who's died.

He himself is planing on living. He's covered a lot of ground since the old days, when he slept in the streets and poked around in dumpsters for food. He says he'll never try suicide again.

His life is far from easy. Hardly anyone's is. But he seems, in some fundamental way, to have been healed.

"Angie was a bitch and everything," he says. "But she was the only one that could tell me, 'Shut the fuck up,' and I would. She believed in me when I didn't believe in me. We all felt that way. She believed in us."

"She was my gay mother, my friend. She put so much shit in my head, just the slap of love. And it woke me up."

After I finished writing this, several months after Dorian's death, a few of her former children were going through her sewing room looking for Halloween costumes when they found a trunk that contained a mummified human body. It was wrapped in strips of leatherette and covered with baking soda. It proved to be the corpse of a black man in his thirties, who had died of gunshot wounds and who had been dead more than twenty years (which meant the body had been moved out of and into several different apartments). Pinned to the body was a note that said, "This poor soul broke into my apartment and I was forced to shoot him."

Nothing more is known, although the discovery did get Dorian's picture on the cover of *New York Magazine*, under the words, "The Drag Queen Had a Mummy in Her Closet."

Ah, Dorian. One last dramatic gesture, from beyond the grave.

"***Entire contents from** *Architectural Digest: The International Magazine of Fine Interior Design*, **September 1993.**"
(Moody, p.83)

Endnotes

OPEN CITY WOULD LIKE TO HEAR FROM YOU. SO WE ARE STARTING A letters column where you can say what you want about the magazine, or any particular piece of writing in it. The idea was inspired by a letter to the editor written by a disgruntled contributor several years ago. She had submitted a story and we had not responded. She then sent in a note about the story, to which we did not respond. Our silence was not out of malice. We were more disorganized then. The contributor then sent in a very long letter in which she outlined what was wrong with our magazine and why we were, more or less, the scum of the earth, and which also went into a lot of detail about how good the story she had submitted was. This prompted us to find the story. The letter was much better than the story. And now we have lost the letter. But if we found it we would print it

More on letters: Alfred Chester's correspondence with Paul Bowles appeared in *Open City #3.* Chester wrote stories and novels, and was a brilliant essayist and critic, but the letters he wrote to Bowles comprised some of his best work. We hoped at the time that we would make a habit out of printing correspondence, but it's proven difficult to locate really good letters and then get whomever has the rights to them to let us print them. Now we're interested in your letters to and from anyone. We'll consider them like we would a story or poem. One important thing: since most people are in possession of letters written to them by other people, please confirm that it's alright to print the letters you're sending us if they were written by someone other than yourself. And please do not send us original copies.

please send all correspondence to:
OPEN CITY 225 Lafayette Street, suite 1114 New York, NY 10012